Cocaine Cowboys

A Jesse McDermitt Novel

Tropical Adventure Series
Volume 3

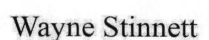

Wayne Stinnett

DOWN ISLAND PRESS

Library of Congress cataloging-in-publication Data

Stinnett, Wayne

Cocaine Cowboys/Wayne Stinnett

p. cm. - (A Jesse McDermitt novel)

ISBN: 978-1-956026-84-9

Cover and graphics by Aurora Publicity

Edited by Marsha Zinberg, The Write Touch

Final Proofreading by Donna Rich

Interior Design by Aurora Publicity

Published by Down Island Press, LLC

If you'd like to receive my newsletter, please sign up on my website.

WWW.WAYNESTINNETT.COM.

Once or twice a month, I'll bring you insights into my private life and writing habits, with updates on what I'm working on, special deals I hear about, and new books by other authors that I'm reading.

The Gaspar's Revenge Ship's Store is open.

ALSO BY WAYNE STINNETT

The Jerry Snyder Caribbean Mystery Series

Wayward Sons   Vodou Child   Friends of the Devil

The Charity Styles Caribbean Thriller Series

Merciless Charity	Enduring Charity	Elusive Charity
Ruthless Charity	Vigilant Charity	Liable Charity
Reckless Charity	Lost Charity	

The Jesse McDermitt Tropical Adventure Series16

A Seller's Market   Bad Blood   Cocaine Cowboys

The Jesse McDermitt Caribbean Adventure Series

Fallen Out	Rising Storm	Steady as She Goes
Fallen Palm	Rising Fury	All Ahead Full
Fallen Hunter	Rising Force	Man Overboard
Fallen Pride	Rising Charity	Cast Off
Fallen Mangrove	Rising Water	Fish On!
Fallen King	Rising Spirit	Weigh Anchor
Fallen Honor	Rising Thunder	Swift and Silent
Fallen Tide	Rising Warrior	Apalach Affair
Fallen Angel	Rising Moon	Dominica Blue
Fallen Hero	Rising Tide	Down Island

Rainbow of Collars Motivational Non-fiction Series

Blue Collar to No Collar   No Collar to Tank Top

Dedicated to Sergeant Bill Ross
From the motor pool, to the PT field, to exploring the Outer Banks by boat,
you were always a great inspiration.
Semper Fi.

"In the Marine Corps, your buddy is not only your classmate or fellow officer, but he is also the Marine under your command. If you don't prepare yourself to properly train him, lead him, and support him on the battlefield, then you're going to let him down.
That is unforgivable in the Marine Corps."
—Chesty Puller

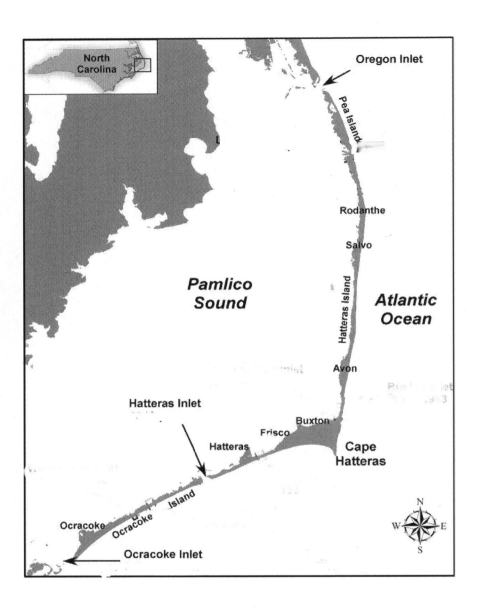

Chapter One

━━━◆━◆━◆━◆━━━

Wilmington, North Carolina
Thursday, March 13, 1980

Ringo Thomas sat at the end of the bar, nursing a now-warm draft beer. It was his usual spot, near the hall that went back to the bathrooms and right next to a large window, through which he could look out and see his boat tied up in its slip. Most important was the pay phone mounted on the wall right next to the window.

Ringo considered himself the epitome of the modern-day pirate. He owned a business that was thriving in his absence, while he played fast and loose with the law, using his highly modified Cigarette racing boat to move drugs into the country.

He'd been waiting several hours for a call, and now that it was getting close to sundown, he had to start thinking about alternative ways to entertain his crew and maybe make some money, if the call he was waiting for didn't come soon.

He'd managed to drink only three beers in the last three-

and-a-half hours, and he'd just put in an order for a cheese-burger and fries, so he could wait a little longer. Miss the call, miss the load. And Ringo pocketed over $100,000 every time the phone rang and he delivered a load.

But they never called after six.

Ringo didn't like waiting. It set him on edge. Even back in his previous life, waiting for a call or fax that would seal a development deal, he'd eventually become what he called "wangry," a type of anger that stemmed from having to wait needlessly.

"Gonna be a long night?" the bartender asked. "Where's your two friends?"

Janet Chapman had been working at Ringo's neighborhood bar for three years and he knew she was actually asking about Tim, not both Tim and Moose.

"They're down getting the boat ready," he replied. "We might get a run tonight."

Janet knew what the three did for a living, but she was one of very few who did. She and Ringo's best friend, Tim Berkowitz, had been having an on-and-off relationship since the eighth grade and currently they were on again.

The pay phone behind him rang, jolting Ringo upright. Janet's eyes cut to it in surprise.

Ringo went to the phone and intercepted some guy who was reaching for it.

"That's for me," he told the guy, then picked up the receiver and held it to his ear until the stranger was gone. "Mel's Seafood."

"Please hold for a ship-to-shore call," a woman's voice said.

Ringo waited and heard a series of clicks as the connection

he'd been waiting for was made, and then the operator said, "Go ahead with your call, captain."

"Mel, can you hear me?" a static-filled voice asked. "Over."

Knowing that the operator was listening, Ringo and the ship's captain had to communicate in a prearranged code.

"Loud and clear, Tony," Ringo said, using the captain's alias. "Are y'all catching anything? Over."

"I have a full fish-box for you, Mel. Same prices as last week's catch. If you're interested, you'll get the first 250-pound pick of what we caught. Say the word and we'll be at your dock at sunrise. Over."

Ringo didn't have a dock and "Tony" wasn't coming to him, and he was pretty sure that wasn't even his name. In fact, the guy he was talking to was the captain of a freighter that carried goods from South America up to New York, not a fishing boat. Ringo understood what he was saying, though.

Their meeting place was always the same—twenty miles due east of Wrightsville Beach—and Tony was saying he'd be at that position at sunrise, and that Ringo would be getting the first full load, a hundred kilos, which, along with the packaging, would weigh 250 pounds.

He also knew it meant taking his prized Cigarette racing boat out into the Atlantic before dawn to meet the freighter twenty miles offshore at sunrise, then slowly meandering up the coast with it, riding the Gulf Stream until right before sunset, just to make sure the law didn't follow him out to the meet.

These guys were careful. And they were also cutthroats.

"Sure thing, Tony," Ringo replied. "Be more than happy to take the first of your catch. And last week's price is great. Over."

"See you in the morning, Mel," the captain said. "Over and out."

Ringo hung up the phone and went back to the bar, already going over everything in his head. They'd need food and water for the whole day, since it'd be close to midnight before they got back.

The tanks were already full of high-octane gas, both engines had been serviced just a month earlier, and he'd changed out a partially frayed fanbelt just the day before and corrected the misaligned pulley that had caused it to wear.

"Was that it?" Janet asked.

He nodded. "How much longer on the burger?"

She turned and looked through the window to where the *real* Mel was flipping onions on the griddle.

"Patties aren't even on yet," she said, turning back to him. "Prolly like ten minutes."

"Keep it warm," he told her. "I gotta run down to the boat."

He walked out of the small diner to the outdoor seating area, which was twice as large, then down the steps to the dock.

When he got to his boat, the hood was open, and Tim was leaning over one of the engines.

"Don't tell me something's wrong," he said, stepping down into the aft cockpit. "I just got the call."

"It's only a loose wire on the oil pressure sending unit," Tim replied, glancing up at him. "I sent Moose up to the truck to get my toolbox. I'll put a new clip on it, heat-shrink the connection, and she'll be good to go." He stood and looked over the engine bay at Ringo. "What time?"

"Pick up the freighter at sunrise," he replied. "Same thing, twenty miles offshore, then follow the ship all day. We're getting the first load and going into Pamlico Sound."

"Cool," Tim said, nodding. "Easiest run of the three. But man, idling all day when we do this shit is gonna severely cut the lifespan of these engines."

"Get that loose wire done, then you guys meet me back here at five tomorrow morning." He pulled a ten from his wallet and handed it to Tim. "Tell Janet that Moose can have my burger."

"Where you goin'?"

"Gotta grab some supplies, and I've got a few things to take care of," Ringo said, as he started back down the dock. He turned his head and called over his shoulder, "Don't stay up late, Tim."

"Yes, Mom," his buddy called back.

When he reached the parking lot, Ringo jumped into his Dodge pickup and headed home, just a few blocks away. His choice of wheels had more to do with blending in than actually carrying anything in the bed of the truck. The car he drove when he was at his other house and commuting to his office was a Corvette. Ringo preferred to keep a low profile when he was at his marina home.

He'd be gone all day tomorrow, so he had to make sure the dogs had plenty of food and water.

Zeus and Chleo had the run of the house as well as the fully fenced yard around it. A former girlfriend had criticized the size of the dog door he'd installed, saying any burglar could probably crawl through it.

"Only halfway," he'd told her. "Zeus would eat his head before he got all the way in."

The two Dobermans had been with him for four years, since

they were both pups. At nearly ninety pounds, Zeus was much bigger than his sister. But Chleo was more agile and athletic, and she could outrun any man, no matter how scared and jacked up on adrenaline they were. Both dogs were "uncut," having natural ears and tails, and were often mistaken for friendly hound dogs.

The supplies for the trip wouldn't be anything fancy, since there wasn't any way to cook on the boat. But he had a good stock of canned beef stew. The cans could be warmed just by placing them next to one of the engines' exhaust manifolds.

He pulled into the short driveway and stopped at the recessed gate with its "Beware of Dogs" sign. The concrete driveway extended another fifty feet beyond the gate to the garage door, and the short part of the pad that was outside the fence made it possible for him to get out and open the gate without blocking the street.

The dogs met him at the driveway gate, both wagging their tails and dancing around. He opened the gate and stepped inside, petting the muscular flanks of his dogs.

"Go to the porch," he ordered them.

They dutifully ran to the front porch and Ringo opened the gates, knowing they'd stay there. He swung both sides all the way open, then got back in his truck and pulled it right up to the garage door.

Once he'd gotten out of the truck and closed the gates, he went to the front porch and looked at the two dogs, both sitting in front of the door, heads and ears up, fully alert.

"Anything happen while I was gone?" he asked.

Chleo whined slightly, turning to look at Zeus for a second, as if waiting for her big brother to respond.

"Well," he said, drawing the word out, "then I guess a *bone* might be in order. If you've both been good."

Chleo yipped slightly, rising to her feet, then sitting back down again as Zeus waited.

Though they were exactly the same age, or at least within minutes, their personalities couldn't be more different. Zeus had taken to the physical training a lot better, but Chleo was obviously more intelligent.

Together, with Zeus's enormous strength and size, and Chleo's unmatched speed and perception, they were very formidable guard dogs.

He unlocked the door and opened it. "Come."

The dogs turned and followed him into the house, where he headed straight to the kitchen and got two large dog chews from a jar in the pantry and gave them each one.

Then the phone rang. He went to the desk in the living room and picked up the receiver. "Hello?"

"Glad I caught you, man," a voice said. "It's Roy, up in Hatteras."

"Hey, Roy. What's up?"

"You mentioned a couple of weeks ago, you might be interested in doing some horse-tradin' for a bigger boat. Still interested?"

Ringo had piled up a mountain of cash in the last two years, mostly from hauling stuff in his boat. But his business was booming, and he didn't even need to be there anymore. He had enough to last several lifetimes in a less expensive part of the world.

He'd been planning to disappear in the not-too-distant

future, and that would mean not just a different boat, but a complete change in identity and lifestyle.

Slow and under the radar, he thought. That's the only way to leave the mob. He drove high-speed boats and that was what his business was centered on. They'd never think he'd disappeared on a slow boat to China.

"Might be," he replied. "Depends on what it is."

"I got a friend a few miles south of here," Roy said. "His brother's got a really nice long-distance cruiser and he's a few months behind on the payments. The bank's gonna take it if he doesn't come up with at least five grand by the end of the month."

"I'm not interested in bailing anyone out of a financial problem," Ringo said. "How big? And how far can it go?"

"My buddy said it's a fifty-some-odd-foot trawler with twin diesels," Roy replied. "You're the first one I thought of, so I asked him what its range was, and get this, with *both* engines running, and cruising at six or seven knots, she can go more than a thousand miles."

A thousand miles? he thought.

Something like that could cross an ocean with just a couple of stops.

"Is it available to look at tomorrow night?" Ringo asked, very interested. "I can be there around nine or so, maybe."

"No can do tomorrow, man," Roy replied. "Dude's out of town till the next day."

He thought about it for a moment. They'd have to stay the night, and head back the next night. The run home was no big deal, just over two hours at a moderate sixty miles an hour. But he'd have to get Janet to check on the dogs.

"Do you have a place to stash my boat and for three of us to crash for the night? Beer's on me."

"I know just the place for the boat," Roy said. "Less than half a mile from my place, and y'all can stay with me."

"Set up the place and time to see the boat," Ringo said, already thinking of faraway beaches. "Then call me back. But make it soon, I'm leaving before sunup."

"I'll make it happen, man," Roy said. "If you don't hear from me before you head out, just come to my place. I'll be waiting and can take you over to my uncle's. He's got a covered boathouse."

Ringo hung up the phone and started packing supplies as his mind turned toward the boat, and how it'd let him escape. He liked all the fun things the extra money allowed, the fast cars, plenty of women, and all the excitement a man could handle, but lately, he felt like his time was running out.

Chapter Two

———◆———◆———◆———◆———

Camp Lejeune, North Carolina
Friday, March 14, 1980

The air was cold, as evidenced by the streams of vapor coming from the nostrils of the men standing in morning formation. Clouds of vapor rose into the clear blue sky—a combination of collective heavy breathing and cooling body temperatures after the three-mile run that the platoon had just finished.

It wasn't frigid cold—not like they'd endured the previous month in Upstate New York. The six weeks that the Eighth Marine Regiment had spent at Fort Drum, along with several other elements of the Second Marine Division, had been an eye-opener for some, particularly the two Marines in Alpha Platoon from Florida, Lance Corporals Jesse McDermitt and Rusty Thurman.

"Colder'n a well-digger's ass," Rusty had proclaimed on their first night in the deep snow of Upstate New York.

During the six weeks of rigorous training, the men in First Battalion, Eighth Marines never saw the inside of a building, unless you counted the two-man shelter halves where they slept or the outdoor showers they bathed in.

It was mid-March, springtime in the Southeast, and Fort Drum was becoming a distant memory. The crepe myrtles in front of the barracks were just starting to show new buds, which, in another couple of weeks, would become bright green leaves.

"McDermitt! Thurman!" the new platoon sergeant called out. "Your leave commences at 0900. Pick up your paperwork from the S-1 clerk before you leave."

"Aye-aye," the two young men shouted in unison.

"Everyone else, turn to for field day. Inspection's at 0900. Platoon! Ah-ten-shun! Fall out!"

The men broke up, most headed back to their rooms to shower and begin cleaning. Field day meant removing nearly everything from the three- and four-man rooms, scrubbing walls, floors, the entire head, and removing the rug and beating it free of dust and dirt before cleaning everything and moving it all back inside.

Their room consisted of two sets of bunk beds, four desks, and four chairs. One of their roommates had a TV in the back of his wall locker that came out on weekends and after hours.

Field day was usually followed by a "junk on the bunk" inspection, but this time, Staff Sergeant O'Brian was only inspecting cleanliness of the rooms, and not each Marine's 782 gear, which included everything they were issued for combat.

"How cold ya think the water's gonna be?" Rusty asked, as they walked toward the Company HQ.

Jesse shrugged. "I doubt Sergeant Livingston would tell us to buy thick wetsuits if it's gonna be balmy. Besides, it won't be colder than Drum—if it is, the surf would freeze."

Rusty chuckled. "That brings a whole new meanin' to the term 'permanent wave.'"

Jesse caught Lance Corporal Walkley's attention and motioned her over. Linda was the clerk for the S-1, Lieutenant Brooks, who was also the company executive officer, or XO.

"Do you have our leave papers ready?" Jesse asked her.

She smiled at him. "The XO has them on his desk to sign."

"He ain't signed 'em yet?" Rusty asked.

Linda and Jesse had planned to go out several times but often, their plans were canceled due to one or both having duty. But they had gone on two short dates.

"Lieutenant Brooks likes to wait til right before," she replied to Rusty. "Just in case."

"In case of what?" Rusty pressed.

"In case you trip over your own feet and have to spend a week in sick bay, Thurman," a voice from behind them said. "Or in case… I don't know… we're put on *alert*. And just why do you feel the need to question my orders?"

Both Marines snapped to attention. "Sorry, sir," Rusty said. "We're just anxious to get under way."

"Come into my office for a minute," he said, lifting the counter's walk-through and moving past Linda. "Get me a coffee, Walkley?"

"Yes, sir," she replied, a slight grimace on her face.

Linda had told Jesse once that fetching coffee was one of her least- liked duties. She'd wanted to be in Motor Transport or some other non-combat MOS that got her outside.

Jesse and Rusty followed the lieutenant back to his office and stood at attention in front of his desk.

"At ease," Brooks ordered. "Have a seat."

When they sat down, Brooks moved two files in front of him, opening each, then signing two pages and handing them to each man.

"Here's your leave papers," Brooks said. "You're to report back here no later than 0600 on Monday, 31 March to begin checking out."

He removed two more sheets, which he signed.

"I won't be here when you get back," he said. "I'm reporting to San Diego the end of next week. These are your orders to report for the Basic Reconnaissance Course on Monday, 7 April, one week after you get back from leave. You'll spend that week checking out and getting to California."

He handed Rusty his and was about to do the same with Jesse's, but paused and looked down at the folder he'd taken it from.

"Says here your birthday's coming up next week, McDermitt."

"Yes, sir," Jesse replied. "On the twentieth."

Brooks looked up at him. "You're only seventeen?"

"Until next Thursday, sir," Jesse replied. "Is that a problem?"

Brooks handed him the orders. "No. It's just that I don't think anyone your age has ever been accepted to Recon School before."

"Don't worry about me, sir," Jesse said. "I won't let you down."

"I'll be right there beside you two during much of BRC," Brooks said. "They make no distinction in rank at the school."

"With all due respect, sir," Rusty began with a grin, "I seen your PFT score. You'll be ahead of both of us."

Lieutenant Brooks was a gifted athlete and had played starting tight end at University of Alabama.

"Not by much," Brooks replied. "I saw both your scores, as well."

The Marine Corps Physical Fitness Test was an annual event that all Marines went though. It consisted of pullups, sit-ups, and a timed three-mile run. Jesse and Brooks were the only two in the platoon who'd maxed the PFT, and Rusty had only missed it by a few sit-ups. But he'd still scored in the top one percent of the platoon.

The lieutenant handed them each a ticket. "Don't lose these. They're your airline tickets. You'll be flying commercial on Friday, 4 April from Jacksonville to Atlanta, then on to San Diego from there. Any questions?"

"No, sir," they both replied.

"Get out of my hootch."

They both quickly stood at attention. "Aye-aye, sir."

When they reached their room, their two roommates were already moving stuff outside. So, they stashed their orders in their wall lockers and pitched in.

As three of them worked, they alternated turns in the shower, getting everything finished and back inside ten minutes before the inspection.

"You guys get out of here," Johnson said, placing his cover on the pillow on his rack.

Johnson and Webster were both wearing "cammies," the new camouflage utility uniform, but Jesse and Rusty were in civilian clothes, or "civvies."

"Our leave doesn't start for ten minutes," Jesse replied.

"If you're still here when the gunny gets here," Webster said, "you're leave ain't startin' till he's finished. Get the hell outta here, man. We got your six."

Jesse and Rusty looked at one another, then quickly grabbed their bags and folders with their orders and tickets from their wall lockers.

"Thanks, guys," Rusty said, as they headed out the door.

"The car all set?" Jesse asked, as they headed toward the front of the barracks and the parking lot.

Rusty had fixed up and sold the Mustang Jesse'd given him several months earlier. Though Jesse had tried to refuse, Rusty had insisted on giving him part of the money and had then used the rest to buy an old Fairlane.

Jesse had put the money with the rest of his stash to give to his grandfather—repayment for the car that was torched.

"New oil pan and valve cover gaskets last weekend when you had duty, and she ain't leakin' no more," he replied. "Changed the oil and filters, too. And I got word of a guy up in Morehead City who has a big block for sale."

"Which route are we taking?" Jesse asked.

Rusty handed him a folded map. "It's open to the parts we'll need, front and back."

Jesse was looking down at the map as he rounded the corner of the building and almost ran into Linda.

"Glad I caught you," she said, pulling up quickly. "You have mail."

He took the envelope from her without looking at it. "Thanks. Are you still thinking of coming out to Sergeant

Livingston's? I called him, and he said you're welcome to join us."

"If I can," she said. "I already know I can't this weekend, but maybe next."

"I hope you do," Jesse called, as she turned and headed back toward the office's entrance.

Walking toward the parking lot, Jesse watched as Linda went along the front of the building. Just before she went inside, she looked back, and he waved.

Rusty looked over his shoulder. "Who you wavin' at?"

"Linda," he replied, as they crossed the street. "She looked back just before she went inside."

"Yep, you're in the deep end, bro."

"What the hell's that supposed to mean?" Jesse asked.

"It's like this," Rusty said, putting the key in the trunk lock and turning it. "You wait for her to look back and she does. She sees you looking and knows she's got the hook set good. Then, just like on New Year's—"

"Don't say it," Jesse said, tossing his bag in the trunk. "I'd prefer to never hear her name again."

Jesse had sort of been dating a girl in the Keys named Gina Albert for several months. They'd spent a week together in The Bahamas late the previous summer, then another week together in the Keys for the New Year celebration.

Then, not two weeks later, just before Jesse deployed to Fort Drum, she'd called and told him that she'd met someone and was taking a job in Texas to be closer to him.

"Yeah, well, uh," Rusty stammered, then tossed his bag in and closed the trunk. "Sergeant Livingston says take the scenic route— Highway 24, to Highway 70, to Highway 12. He says it's shorter and faster. But it's still more'n a hundred miles and it's gonna take us a good four hours. Should be okay on gas, though. I just filled her up yesterday."

"That's a long time for just a hundred miles," Jesse said. "That's only twenty-five miles per hour."

"We'll only be drivin' one and a half," Rusty said opening the driver's door. "The Ocracoke Ferry ride's two and a half hours."

"That'll be fun," Jesse said.

"Cool, bro. *Kids* have fun."

"It'll be cool then," Jesse said with a grin.

Rusty got in the driver's seat and waited till Jesse got in the other side. "Sergeant Livingston said he ain't gonna be back to the dock till just before sunset anyway, so there ain't no rush."

"Sunset's about 1800," Jesse said. "What do we do for the other five hours once we get off the ferry?"

"That's why they call it a scenic route, bro," Rusty said, starting the engine. "Check the map for some cool things to stop and check out."

Jesse glanced at the map. "Head for the Snead's Ferry gate," he said, then began tracing a finger along Highway 24. "Hey, Morehead City's right on the way."

"Is 'at right?" Rusty asked, backing out of the parking spot. "Well, if that don't beat all."

Chapter Three

◆————◆——◆——◆——◆

Traffic was light for a Friday. It was midmorning on a cool spring workday, so that wasn't much of a surprise in the rural parts of coastal North Carolina. Most people were where they were going to be for the biggest part of their day—working.

Jesse felt a rush of freedom. His normal day-to-day activities revolved around his duties and training as an infantry Marine. But for the next week, he and Rusty had no responsibilities, and nobody but their command knew where they were, except Rusty's girlfriend Juliet, back home in the Florida Keys, and she was happy that Rusty was taking time for himself.

While in the frigid north, he and Rusty had talked at length with their platoon sergeant about treasure hunting and diving, and their planned weekends in the Outer Banks quickly became a whole week, and then two.

Rusty and Jesse had only taken two leave periods of the month they were allotted every year, and with their one-year anniversary of stepping on the yellow footprints approaching, they were advised to use the remaining leave they had before then.

The Corps didn't like lower-ranked enlisted personnel saving up leave time.

Sergeant Livingston was currently on a month-long leave with his family before he'd report to Okinawa, Japan for a one-year unaccompanied tour, meaning he'd be leaving his wife and young son at home.

Jesse had met Suzanne Livingston a couple of times and found her to be friendly and easy to talk to, kind of like an older sister. When he'd run into her at the base exchange the week before Sergeant Livingston went on leave, she'd seemed excited to have company at their house on Ocracoke Island, but Jesse still felt as if they were intruding on family time.

They rode with the windows down, the car's heater blowing just a little warm air on their feet, and wore light jackets against the chill air blowing in through the windows.

"Who was the letter from?" Rusty asked when he stopped at a light.

"Oh, I forgot all about it," Jesse said, twisting to reach his hip pocket.

"Do tell," Rusty said with a smirk. "Wouldn't have anything to do with bumping into that little redheaded Ice Queen, would it?"

"She's not like that, and you know it," Jesse said, looking at the envelope. "It's from Pap."

"Well, open it. What's he say?"

"I worry whenever I get a letter from one of them," Jesse said, looking down at the envelope.

"Hell they ain't *that* old, bro."

"Pap's going to be sixty-four in July," Jesse replied. "And Mam will be fifty-eight next month."

"'Sides, he wouldn't tell you bad news in a letter," Rusty said. "I met him just that once, but he didn't strike me that way."

"I know," Jesse said, tearing the end of the envelope, pulling out a single handwritten page, and reading it.

It was written on stationary from Pap's former business. He still had reams of it in his little office out in the garage, though he'd sold the business nearly ten years ago.

Rusty glanced over. "What's he say?"

"He says Mam is going on a cruise with some of the ladies from church next week," Jesse replied. "Says he was thinking of coming up to Jacksonville for my birthday."

"You didn't tell him we were goin' to the Outer Banks?"

Jesse looked back down at the letter again. "I thought they might be upset if I didn't come home for my leave."

"Well, you're gonna have to tell him soon," Rusty said. "You'd better call him as soon as we get there."

They rode in silence for a while. Jesse thought about his grandfather being alone for a whole week and felt even more guilt-ridden.

A little more than an hour after leaving Camp Lejeune, Rusty turned off the highway at a junkyard on the outskirts of Morehead City.

"I called the guy yesterday," he said, climbing out of the Fairlane coupe. "He said he'd have it on a pallet, drained."

"You're buying a new motor now?" Jesse asked, walking toward what could pass for an office. "Where are you going to put it?"

"It's just a short block," Rusty replied. "No heads, no intake, no exhaust manifolds, and no oil pan. Just the block and the rotating assembly. It'll fit in the trunk."

"You're going to haul an engine in the trunk of the car all the way to the Outer Banks and back?"

"Ya snooze, ya lose," Rusty said. "This motor came out of a wrecked school bus."

"A school bus?" Jesse asked, as they approached the office.

On closer inspection, the building looked abandoned and was leaning slightly. But then the door opened, and a stooped old man came out, lighting a cigarette. His face was wrinkled and weathered, and his hair under a John Deere hat was snowy white.

"Let me do the talkin'," Rusty said, then waved to the man. "Are you Mr. Snodgrass?"

He eyed them suspiciously. "Depends on who's askin'."

"Rusty Thurman," he replied. "I talked to ya on the phone about a big block Ford motor for a Winnebago."

"Oh, yeah," the old man said, then waved for them to follow him. "I got it back here in the dry barn."

The "dry barn" was more of a lean-to with three walls and an open front. Inside were dozens of pallets with car parts on them.

"Here ya go," the man said, stopping beside a pallet. "School bus motor. You look awful young to be an RVer."

"It's for my dad's camper," Rusty replied, bending to inspect the serial number stamped into the block. "His old motor sucked a valve headin' back from Arizona, and I'm gonna build him a new one before he and my mom go west again in the fall. Got a rag?"

Snodgrass pulled a dirty rag from the back of his jeans and

handed it to him. Rusty bent again and rolled the engine onto its side a little, so he could wipe the sludge and grime from the plate.

Jesse noticed his friend's eyes widen when he saw the bottom of the engine.

"Yep," Rusty said, "it's an FE, alright. You said fifty bucks?"

"I got the heads too," Snodgrass said. "Another fifty."

"Thanks, but we won't need 'em," Rusty said, straightening and handing over the cash. "The valve didn't hurt the head none and they're both at the machine shop already."

"Good enough," the old man said, as he stuffed the bills in his pocket. "You haulin' it in that car of yours? I ain't got no lift or nothin', but back on in here and maybe the three of us can get it in the trunk."

A moment later, Rusty backed the Fairlane up to the opening and, after moving their bags, new wetsuits, and dive gear to the backseat, he and Jesse had no trouble lifting the heavy engine into the trunk.

"Pleasure doin' business with ya," Snodgrass said, as they got back in the car.

Jesse waved as Rusty pulled the car away from the dry barn, heading back out to the gate.

Rusty waited for two cars to pass before pulling out.

"A bus engine?" Jesse asked again. "For a Winnebago?"

"Never show your cards when it comes to motors," he replied. "If that guy knew I was buildin' a hot rod, he'd have upped the price." He paused, then looked over and grinned as he shifted to third gear. "Big block FE motors have been used in a lot of Ford cars and trucks since the early sixties, bro. Same block that's in a lot of dump trucks, cargo vans, and station wagons. But this one's an R-code, which was used in the Boss Mustang; just different heads and pistons."

"Something on the bottom of the motor told you that?"

Rusty grinned again. "Glad he didn't catch that," Rusty said, a note of triumph in his voice. "The man didn't know what he had. R-code motors have cross-bolted main bearings. How one ended up in a school bus, I ain't got a clue. But I'm thinkin' I could build one that'll do over four hundred horses. And when it comes to torque, there ain't no replacement for displacement."

Rusty continued extolling the virtues of the big-block Ford engines for several miles, while Jesse looked out the window, occasionally catching a glimpse of the water.

"Coming into Beaufort," Jesse said noticing a road sign. "Just follow 70 through town."

"*Bo*-furt," Rusty corrected. "It's actually the right way to say it, but folks down in *South* Carolina, where PI is, call it *Bew*-furt."

"There's a McDonald's," Jesse said, pointing ahead. "And there's a pay phone outside the C-store next door. I can call Pap."

"Perfect," Rusty said, slowing the car. "We need to put some ice into that cooler in the back seat."

He pulled in and parked the car. "I'll go get us some chow. You got enough change?"

"No, I'll have to get change at the store," Jesse replied.

Rusty went inside, while Jesse went to the convenience store to get ice and change. Once he'd put the ice in the cooler, he went out to the pay phone to make the call.

"Hello?" Pap said, after just one ring.

He was sitting in his den, Jesse guessed, where there was a second phone right beside his recliner.

"Hey, Pap. It's me."

Jesse recognized a whoosh of air as Pap sat up in the chair, which for some reason made Jesse smile.

"Everything okay?" he asked.

"Yeah, Pap, everything's fine. I just got your letter."

When Rusty came out with the food a few minutes later, Jesse was still on the phone, so he walked over, but Jesse was just saying goodbye and hung up.

"What'd he say?" Rusty asked, as they walked across the parking lot to a concrete table in front of the restaurant. "That was a long call for just two bucks."

"That was the *second* one," Jesse said. "I called Sergeant Livingston to see if it was okay for another guest for a few days."

"Your pap's comin'?" Rusty asked in disbelief.

"He'd already booked a flight to Jacksonville," Jesse replied. "I felt bad enough, so I suggested he change it to Ocracoke."

"They got an airport there?"

"Not really an airport," Jesse replied. "Just an airstrip. Pap says he knows a private pilot in Jacksonville that can give him a ride the rest of the way."

"And how's that gonna work out when the Ice Queen arrives?"

Chapter Four

———◆——◆—◆—◆——◆———

J esse fretted over what might happen if Linda *did* come. He knew she couldn't promise to be there. Weekend liberty wasn't like leave, and the whole company could have liberty canceled at any time, even if it was just because the company gunny wanted to get out of the house.

Like many, Linda didn't own a car. If she *was* able to make it, she'd told him that she'd take the bus, since the odds of catching a ride to the Outer Banks with another Marine at Swoop Circle were pretty slim.

Swoop Circle was the unofficial name of a small parking lot behind the Mainside tennis courts at Camp Lejeune. On Fridays, Marines *with* cars met up with others needing a ride for a swoop home or someplace nearby. The riders paid ten or twenty dollars, which was cheaper than a bus ticket, and got them where they were going twice as fast. Some Marines invested in larger cars, or even vans, and turned swooping into a side hustle.

"Cedar Island's just ahead," Rusty said. "That's where we'll catch the ferry to Ocracoke."

Jesse glanced over at him. "Any idea what the schedule is?"

"First one runs at 0700," Rusty replied. "It takes better'n five hours to get there, unload, reload, and get back. So the next one should be around 1300 or so."

Jesse glanced at his watch. It was almost noon, so they were going to have to wait a while.

"There's the sign for Highway 12," Jesse said, as Rusty slowed for a three-way stop. "Hang a left. It's just a few miles away."

"Shouldn't be hard to find," Rusty said, turning and accelerating.

He was right. The road ended at the ferry terminal, where a couple of cars were already lined up in front of the concrete ramp and seawall.

"That looks like where we check in," Jesse said, pointing. "Drop me there and I'll go in and pay, while you pull up behind that last car."

When Rusty stopped, Jesse got out, strolled toward the building, then went inside. Nobody else was in line, so he approached the ticket booth.

"Goin' to Ocracoke?" the woman behind the counter asked.

She was older, probably in her forties or fifties, a little on the heavy side, and had a no-nonsense way about her, from her clothes, to her hairstyle, to her efficient mannerisms.

"Yes, ma'am," he replied. "One car, two passengers."

"What kinda car?"

He pointed out the window. "That blue Ford at the end of the line."

She glanced out for about half a second, pulled a card from a drawer and wrote on it, then placed it on the counter. "That'll be ten-sixty, including tax."

Jesse pulled his wallet out, withdrew a ten and a one and passed them over.

She made the change, handed it to him, and pushed the card across the counter, along with a brochure. "Put this on your dashboard. When the ferry docks, be in your car ready to board. There'll be crew to guide you." She glanced up at a clock on the wall. "Ought to be here in less than an hour."

He thanked her, took the card and brochure, and walked back out into the sunshine.

Rusty was leaning on the front fender of the car when Jesse got there. He reached in and put the card on the dash, then joined his friend, who was looking out over the water.

"Looks big," Jesse said, taking a leaning spot next to him.

"Pamlico Sound," Rusty replied. "Home of the legendary pirate, Edward Teach."

"Never heard of him."

"Yargh," Rusty said with a piratical grin. "Cap'n Teach went by the name *Blackbeard*."

"Now him, I've heard of," Jesse said. "He was from around here?"

Rusty looked out over the water again. "Some stories say he was born here; Ocracoke to be exact. Others say he was from England or was born in Jamaica but grew up in England."

"What do you think?" Jesse asked, his eyes following his friend's gaze. "And how do you know so much about him?"

"How I know is simple," Rusty replied. "My family's lived on that rock of an island called Key Vaca for nearly a hundred and fifty years, so we've heard of every pirate out there and seen a few."

He looked up at Jesse and grinned. "What I think about Teach is that he's still swimmin' around out there lookin' for his head. And when he finds it, the ghost of ol' Captain Maynard better watch out."

"Is that who killed him?" Jesse asked, finding himself being drawn into the story.

"Not by himself," Rusty replied. "Maynard and his crew ambushed Teach, killed him and his whole crew, then cut Teach's head off, and threw his body into the Sound. Legend says they mounted his head to their bowsprit and sailed back to Virginia."

"And all that happened right here?"

"Well, not *here*, here," Rusty said, pointing out over the water. "It happened just off Ocracoke Island. Prolly twenty miles from here, though."

Jesse looked in that direction and saw something on the horizon. "Is that the ferry?"

Rusty put a hand over his brow to shade his eyes. "'Bout three miles out. Could be it."

As the boat got closer, it became obvious that it was the ferry.

"It's bigger'n I thought," Rusty said.

Jesse opened the brochure and looked it over. "Says here it can carry twenty cars and a hundred passengers."

Rusty let out a low whistle as another car pulled in behind them. They both looked back as a man got out of a newer-looking four-door Chevy Impala and walked toward the office. A woman sat in the front passenger seat, and there were two kids in back, a girl and a boy, no more than seven to nine, with the boy obviously older.

Behind the Impala, two more cars pulled in and lined up.

"Looks like we got here about the right time," Rusty said.

They'd be the third car to load, once the ferry unloaded, and over the next twenty minutes more cars arrived.

Finally, the ferry stopped and turned completely around before backing up to the dock. The name *Sea Level* was painted on the stern, and there were two rows of cars on her deck and several people standing around them.

The crew was efficient, and the drivers were ready, so in ten minutes, all the cars were off, and they started reloading.

Rusty drove carefully across the ramp, following hand signals from two crewmen, and when they reached the other end of the ferry, he parked closely behind the same car that they'd waited behind to board.

"Two-and-a-half hours to get there," Jesse said, "plus an hour waiting for the ferry. No wonder it takes so long to go just a hundred miles. How long would it take to go around and come in from the north?"

"It's an island, bro," Rusty said. "No bridges on or off. If ya go around, the ferry ride's shorter, but it'd cost more in gas and a longer drive."

They went forward to the wide bow of the boat, where there were several groups of seats, all facing forward. They moved to the center of the front row.

"This is one big-ass boat," Rusty said. "Bigger'n the old ferry that used to run to Marathon. If they get twenty cars on here, it'd be lucky to make two or three hundred bucks a run. Wonder how much fuel the engines burn."

"Says here it's owned by the North Carolina Department of Transportation," Jesse said, looking at the pamphlet again. "And it's the second Cedar Island ferryboat to carry the name *Sea Level*."

Most of the passengers chose to ride inside, out of the cool air. But the couple with the two kids soon came forward and sat down a few feet away from them.

The sounds of the cars' engines soon died down and the ferry's whistle blew loudly. Then it started pulling away from the dock and Jesse could hear a good deal of splashing as the prop wash met the seawall far behind them.

"Twenty miles in two-and-a-half hours," Jesse began, "means we'll only be going eight miles per hour."

"Seven knots," Rusty corrected. "If you're ever gonna be a true waterman, instead of a landlubber who goes out on boats, ya gotta understand the lingo."

"So, a knot is one less than a mile per hour?" Jesse asked, punking his friend.

"Just to make it easy, there's roughly 0.88 nautical miles in a statute mile, or 1.15 statute miles in a nautical."

"So ten knots is eleven and a half miles per hour?"

Rusty nodded. "Simple math."

The ferry began to gather speed, and Jesse could hear the bow wave just below the rail ahead of them. He rose and went forward, but the bow was farther back, and he couldn't see the waves.

They were headed roughly east-northeast, as near as he could tell, and the wind over the bow, which he'd noticed earlier was out of the east, was colder now that it had another few knots of boat speed.

Jesse didn't mind it. He figured that no matter where he went for the rest of his life, and whatever time of year that might be, it wasn't going to be as cold as the weeks they'd spent at Fort Drum.

When he returned to his seat, Jesse looked over and caught the young boy with the couple looking at them. He smiled.

"Are you soldiers?" the boy asked.

"We're Marines," Jesse replied. "Soldiers of the sea."

"Like on Gomer Pyle," the father said to his son.

Jesse held his tongue. The guy didn't know any better.

"Sorry," the man said. "We're going to the Outer Banks for vacation, and it's been a long ride already this morning to get here. I'm afraid the kids are a little wound up."

"Where are you coming from?" Jesse asked, just to be polite.

"Florida," he replied. "The Panhandle."

"We're from Florida, too," he said. "I'm from Fort Myers and my friend here is from the Keys."

Rusty leaned forward and looked over at the man. "Where in the Panhandle?"

"A little town nobody's ever heard of," the woman answered. "It's called Quincy, not far from Tallahassee."

"I'm from Marathon," Rusty said. "That's in the Middle Keys."

"I've only heard of Key West and Key Largo," the man said.

"Key West's about a hundred miles from Key Largo," Rusty said. "Largo's in the Upper Keys and Key West's in the Lower Keys, but there's seventeen hundred islands in the Keys altogether."

"I had no idea there were so many," the man said, rising and stepping over to extend his hand.

Rusty and Jesse both stood and shook hands with him.

"I'm Boyd Simpson," he said, then waved a hand at his family. "My wife Jackie, and our kids, Mike and Katy."

"Rusty Thurman," Rusty replied. "And my friend, Jesse McDermitt."

"Are y'all on leave?"

"Yes, sir," Jesse replied. "Going to visit our platoon sergeant on Ocracoke before he ships out to Japan."

"What do you do in the Marines?" the boy asked.

"Don't be so nosy, Mike," his mother admonished.

"That's okay," Rusty said with a grin. "We're in the infantry."

"What's infantry?" he pressed.

Jesse chuckled. "Ground pounders. Air wingers fly around in planes, armor guys ride around in tanks, but we walk."

"How far?"

"To wherever the fightin' is," Rusty replied with a chuckle. "Or wherever they tell us to go to wait for the fightin' to start."

"It's getting cold, Boyd," the mother said, her expression troubled. "Let's go inside."

They quickly retreated to the warmth of the interior of the passenger part of the boat.

"You shouldn't have said that part about the fighting," Jesse said. "I think you scared her."

Rusty shook his head. "That's the trouble with this country. People take freedom for granted, without realizin' what it costs."

Chapter Five

◆ ◆ ◆ ◆

When the ferry approached Ocracoke Island, it entered a narrow inlet into a small lagoon, with dozens of docks sticking out from the homes located around the perimeter.

The cars were all facing the bow, so the ferry didn't need to turn around like it had at the Cedar Island dock. Good thing, too; there was far less maneuvering room.

Jesse and Rusty were still way too early to go straight to Sergeant Livingston's house. He'd told them they could, that his wife and son would be home, but he'd be out on the water until almost sunset.

Neither Jesse nor Rusty felt comfortable going to his house when he wasn't there, so once they drove the car off the ferry, they decided to just park and look around for a while.

The town was small, just a few square miles, and situated around the lagoon, which they learned was called Silver Lake Bay. There were a good many shops and tourist attractions devoted to Blackbeard, as well as quite a few businesses dedicated to sport fishing.

Finally, they got back in the car and followed Highway 12 east, out of the village, toward the beach. The town gave way almost instantly to wetland, and within minutes, they passed the entrance to the airstrip.

"I guess that's where Pap's going to fly into," Jesse said, as the ocean spread out in front of them.

"You oughta call Linda and get her on the plane with your pap," Rusty suggested, as he steered around a left curve to parallel the beach.

Jesse didn't figure Linda hitching a ride with Pap would be a very good idea, and though he couldn't very well uninvite either one, he was beginning to hope Linda couldn't make it.

"He's getting here tomorrow," Jesse said. "Late evening."

Rusty slowed and turned into a parking lot on the right. "Let's check out the beach."

He parked the car in a nearly empty lot, and they both climbed out, getting hit instantly by a stiff breeze off the ocean.

The sun was shining and there wasn't a cloud in the sky, but the wind was bitterly cold, heavy with the taste and scent of the sea.

Jesse zipped up his jacket and looked back across the narrow island toward Pamlico Sound. "We're at least twenty-five miles from the mainland," he said. "And this island isn't even half a mile wide here."

"Folks lived out here long before the ferries came," Rusty said. "I think the first settlers arrived out here in the 1600s. Takes a special breed to survive hurricanes on nothing more than a sandbar."

"Could you imagine?" Jesse said, as they walked toward a

path. "No hurricane warning, no advance notice, just a cloud bank on the horizon."

"By the time they realized how bad it was," Rusty said somberly, "there woulda been no time to jump in a boat and sail across Pamlico Sound."

"That alone would be scary as hell," Jesse said. "Twenty-five miles in a raging storm, with sandbars all around? It'd take half the day."

"Or stay put," Rusty said. "And trust in your construction and people. My family ain't never run from a 'cane."

"I noticed that most of the houses in town were built up and had real shutters," Jesse said. "Guess that's why."

They followed the path toward the beach, then onto a wooden boardwalk that crossed the dune before they stepped out onto the beach itself.

The sand was coarse and a little off-white in color, a bit like Onslow Beach, near the base. The dune was covered with sea oats, swaying with the wind, numerous stunted bushes that had grown as if sculpted by the wind, and a scattering of yuccas, some six feet tall.

Inland, just as along most of coastal Carolina, there were massive live oak trees, many with great sheets of Spanish moss dripping from their branches.

"Primordial," Rusty said, as they walked slowly toward the water, where large waves crashed ashore. "I bet this was the same view old Edward Teach grew up lookin' at. Ain't no wonder he took to the sea."

Jesse looked up and down the coast. "That brochure said that after a storm, parts of old shipwrecks are uncovered, and sometimes things wash ashore."

"Like what?"

"I left it in the car, but there was an older picture that showed the ribs and keel of a wooden ship right on this beach."

They sat down in the sand, facing the ocean, and the wind diminished slightly as it rose to pass over their heads and across the island.

"I've read a lot about this area," Rusty said, having to raise his voice a little to be heard over the surf. "Always wanted to come here. Not Ocracoke in particular, but the whole Outer Banks, ya know. It's shallow out there for quite a ways. Did ya know that the Outer Banks are called the Graveyard of the Atlantic?"

Jesse nodded, pushing the sand with his bare feet. "Treacherous place to be in a storm, I bet."

Once they were on the ferry, both he and Rusty had left their shoes in the car, and though it was cold, neither felt the need to put them back on again.

Rusty swept a hand seaward. "They say there's probably been close to five thousand ships go down along this coast. Most of 'em by storm."

"Five *thousand?*"

Rusty pointed to the south. "See that point stickin' out there? That's Ocracoke Inlet. There's a natural cut to the open ocean out there. Teach and his crew were anchored just inside the inlet when Maynard came sailing through there in a big fat sloop, ridin' low in the water."

Jesse glanced over at him. "A merchant ship?"

Rusty nodded. "Small one, yeah. Kind of an island trader. Old Teach had already received a pardon for piracy, but he couldn't resist the temptation, so he sailed out to rob 'em."

"What happened?"

"The sloop was ridin' low, but not because Maynard had a lot of cargo aboard. When the fight started, his men came rushin' up from the holds, outnumberin' Teach's crew by two to one. They say when his body was examined later, Teach had been shot five times, had more'n twenty saber and knife cuts, and was still fightin' when he went down. That's prolly why they cut off his head—they were *that* scared o' the man."

"Some people are harder to kill," Jesse said. "Pap told me that once, on one of the few occasions he spoke about the war."

"This'll be an interestin' mix," Rusty said. "A World War II vet, a Nam vet, and me and you—a coupla boots, plus the Ice Queen."

"I wish you wouldn't call her that," Jesse said. "She's a nice girl, just a little shy."

Jesse looked out over the water, and far in the distance he could see white water—big ocean waves colliding with a shallow sand bank, he surmised.

He could also see places where there wasn't any surf action.

"See out there where there aren't waves hitting the shallows?" he said to Rusty. "Those must be inlets or cuts through the shallower sand banks."

"Bet ya don't see that in Fort Myers," Rusty said. "When a storm blows, we can see the cuts in the reefs back home the same way."

Jesse scanned the water. "I doubt conditions are ever better than this right now. Those waves come all the way from Africa, and they'd only get bigger during a storm."

Rusty chuckled as he got to his feet. "You'll be a waterman

one day," he said. "Let's go find a store. We don't wanna show up empty-handed."

"There was a liquor store on the edge of town," Jesse said. "We should bring our hostess a bottle of wine."

As they walked back toward the parking lot, Jesse's foot kicked something solid under the sand, and he paused to look back.

"What's the matter?" Rusty asked.

"A board or something under the sand," Jesse replied, squatting to dig around whatever it was. "Some kid could get hurt."

He pulled it free from the sand. Whatever it was, it was heavier than a board, and it was L-shaped, almost a foot long on one side and half that on the other.

"That ain't no board," Rusty said. "Looks like a piece of coral or somethin', but I don't think they's any *hard* corals this far north."

Jesse carried it to the boardwalk and bent over, lightly tapping the end on the bottom step. It crumbled and partly broke away. He grabbed the loosened piece and pried it away, revealing some sort of tube or something.

"It's a pistol!" Rusty exclaimed.

"Who knows?" Jesse said. "Maybe Sergeant Livingston has something to clean it with and get all the barnacles off."

"Put it on the floor in the back," Rusty said, as they started up the boardwalk. "It might be valuable. Pretty good start for a treasure huntin' adventure, huh?"

"If it turns out to be anything of value," Jesse replied, then looked up toward the sky. "It's just a couple of hours to sunset. Think he's back yet?"

"Only one way to find out," Rusty replied. "Let's hit the store, then head on over there."

Chapter Six

———◆——◆——◆——◆——◆———

After visiting the liquor store, Rusty and Jesse stopped at a toy store to get something for Sergeant Livingston's son, who was almost three. It was a wooden puzzle with various shaped blocks that fit into corresponding holes.

The sun was getting low over Pamlico Sound as they followed the directions their platoon sergeant had given them and arrived at a fairly large house on the south side of the village, right on the water.

It sat alone at the end of the street and was elevated about five feet above the ground, with the underside mostly enclosed with boards having a gap of several inches between them.

"Blow out walls," Rusty said. "The gaps let the wind through, but if there's a surge, the boards are sacrificed."

It wasn't a mansion or anything, but it was larger than most of the homes they'd seen in town. The roofline was low, with minimal slope to the peak.

The windows had large, exterior shades, as large as the windows themselves. The shades were propped at an angle to block the sun, and the horizontal slats in them were positioned so they didn't block the wind. It was obvious the shades could be lowered and the slats closed, blocking the window off completely in case of a violent storm or hurricane.

The gravel driveway was long and well-kept, with the house sitting on at least three acres of neatly trimmed grass. A single live oak that stood in the middle shaded more than half the front lawn.

Jesse had noticed as they'd driven down the street that the neighbors' houses were all built up on pilings as well, and all had seemed to have equal floor heights, regardless of the ground level they sat on, the way a high tide line is visible on a seawall.

"That's about the most serious-lookin' storm shelter I ever seen," Rusty said, as they approached the end of the driveway. "See them shutters? I bet they're made of heavy oak planks."

At the end of the driveway was a circle, where a topless, black Jeep was parked next to a newer model, dark-gray Pontiac Bonneville.

"You sure you got the directions right?" Rusty asked. "This looks a little fancy for a sergeant's pay. And I don't see his truck nowhere."

Sergeant Livingston drove an old, beat-up Chevy pickup most of the time. When it was running. On those occasions, his wife dropped him off in her car, the gray Bonneville. So Jesse knew it was the right house.

"I noticed it was still in the parking lot when we left," Jesse said. "But that's his wife's car. I guess the pickup's his daily driver around the base. No idea who owns the Jeep."

Just then, Sergeant Livingston appeared at the side of the

house and waved. He was shirtless, wearing cutoff jeans, his feet were bare, and he had a good ten-day start to a dark beard.

The driveway at the top of the circle, where the two cars were parked, was much wider, and the two cars were parked at an angle, so Rusty pulled the Fairlane up next to the Jeep and they got out.

"Have any trouble finding the place?" Sergeant Livingston asked.

"No trouble at all," Rusty replied. "And a nice ride on the ferry."

"Welcome to Howard House," he said, shaking hands with his two underlings. "Damned glad you could make it. I'm getting closer to the mother lode."

"Thanks, Sergeant," Jesse said. "What do you—"

"If we're gonna have any fun this week," he interrupted, "you have to call me Russ, Jesse. We're on leave and this is another world. Rank and military bearing are left at the Cedar Island dock."

Jesse grinned. "Thanks, Russ. Why 'Howard House?'"

"Because my seventh great-grandfather used to own the whole island," a woman's voice behind Jesse said. "My maiden name was Howard."

The two young men turned to greet Russ's wife. She was strikingly beautiful without even trying. Her blond hair hung past her shoulders, she had a dark tan, and deep blue eyes.

"You remember my wife, Suzanne," Russ said, slipping an arm around her narrow waist. "You met briefly at the Birthday Ball. Honey, these are the two guys I told you about, Rusty Thurman and Jesse McDermitt."

"Please, just call me Suzanne," she said.

The two shook her hand and Rusty asked, "He owned the whole island?"

She nodded. "He was the last to own all of it, and he sold parts of it off for a profit. And before that," she continued with a smile, "he was quartermaster for Blackbeard, his second-in-command."

"No way!" Rusty exclaimed excitedly. "Wait... you said Howard? William Howard?"

Her smile broadened. "Yes! But he left the crew a few months before Blackbeard and his men were killed or captured, then hanged."

"I just got back, honey," Russ said to his wife. "Y'all come out back and I'll show you what I found today."

They started to follow Russ around the house, then Jesse remembered what he'd found on the beach.

"Hang on," he said. "We found something too, and want you to have a look at it."

"Oh?" Russ asked.

Jesse sprinted to the car and got the encrusted artifact from the backseat floorboard and brought it to Russ.

He took it and examined it, paying particular attention to the part Jesse had cracked open.

"This is interesting," he said. "But you shouldn't have broken it. You could have damaged what's inside."

"How else would you get it out?" Jesse asked.

"Follow me," Russ replied, and headed around the corner of the house. "It's time-consuming, but using electrolysis, it can be cleaned up a lot better with less damage."

"Electrolysis?" Jesse asked.

"Using electricity, baking soda, and fresh water," Rusty said, "to break up the rust."

Russ turned and arched an eyebrow. "That's right. You're a bit of a treasure hunter too."

Rusty chuckled. "If ya mean old nails, buttons, and hull spikes, yeah."

Russ led them out into the backyard, which was as expansive as the front. Just off the elevated porch was a sandbox and a wading pool, along with a big charcoal grill, and a table and chairs on a concrete pad.

There was a large utility building that looked fairly new, standing next to a rain cistern that was obviously much older, and towered over the building. A door and two windows were on the nearer side, and a single window at the near end. A long pier extended out from the building, with a boat tied off at the end.

Russ opened the door to the shop and Suzanne entered, with Jesse and Rusty following her.

Inside, there were full-length counters against the two longest walls, with a large sink at the far end, with a window looking out over the sound.

Some of the counters had cabinets under them and the ones that didn't had stuff stored on the floor. One had a small refrigerator or freezer under it, and another, a large air compressor and hoses—a dive tank filling station.

There were wall outlets above the tables about every six or eight feet, and four fluorescent lights down the center of the ceiling.

Both counters were covered with small blue containers, each about two feet long, but there were two very large ones at the ends.

"This is what I brought up today," Russ said, stopping at a plastic tub of clear water.

There was an angled piece of metal standing at one end, part of it out of the water, and an electrical clamp attached to the dry end. At the other end of the tub lay a large clump of what looked like rocks, wrapped with a wire that extended up out of the water and had another electrical clamp attached.

The water was bubbling a fine mist all around the clump, especially where the wire made contact.

"What is it?" Jesse asked, as Russ began winding wire around the thing they'd found on the beach.

"I'm pretty sure it's a bunch of silver coins," Russ replied. "Look at the shape. I think it might be a coin pouch, after the material rotted away, but we won't know for sure until tomorrow morning."

With practiced hands, Russ put the artifact they'd found into an empty tub, then placed another angled piece of metal at the other end.

"What's the angle bracket for?" Jesse asked.

"Sacrificial anode," Rusty replied, watching Russ work. "Like the zincs on an outboard motor."

"Correct again," Russ said with an approving nod. "The electricity will pass through the water from the bracket to the metal in whatever you have here and basically dissolve the rust as the bracket gains rust."

"And when the rust breaks apart," Rusty added, "the barnacles and corals encrustin' the rusty object can be removed a lot easier."

"The end looks like a gun barrel," Jesse noted.

"Possibly," Russ agreed. "Or any kind of metal tube. If it is a pistol, it's a large bore, probably .65 caliber or bigger. "It might take a couple of days and a few baths for this one."

"Was that all you found?" Suzanne asked. "Possible silver coins?"

Russ grinned at his wife. "Would I have brought you out here for a few silly coins?"

She smiled as he moved to the opposite table and down to the other end.

There, in yet another plastic tub, Jesse saw a small object bubbling, which was attached to what looked like a gold chain. Beside it were two coins that also appeared to be gold.

"Is that real gold?" Jesse asked.

"Sure is," Russ replied. "Gold is so dense, nothing can grow on it."

"Those look like the same coins you found the other day," Suzanne said. "And a gold chain?"

Russ smiled and leaned on the table. "That encrustation is some kind of precious gemstone, I think. It'll look good around your neck."

Then he nodded his head to the other side of the room. "Here's a few I found last week."

He reached into a tub and took a coin out, then gently patted it dry with a towel before handing it to Rusty and reaching for another coin.

"These are English guineas," Russ said, handing the second coin to Jesse. "The saline solution is less than seawater, and these are ready to come out. They were minted in 1680, and at the time, worth twenty-one shillings each. That's the image of Charles II. There are twenty shillings per pound. So these would have been worth a little over one English pound, once England established a set value about the turn of the century. Before that, the value of a guinea went up and down with gold prices."

"What are they worth today?" Jesse asked, looking closely at the front of the coin. It showed the profile of a man with a long nose and curly hair to his shoulders.

"That depends," Russ replied. "Each coin is a quarter ounce of gold, so just in melt value, they're worth a good twenty-five bucks. Way more than a British pound. But to a *collector*... I think I can get seven hundred."

Jesse looked up, surprised. "Dollars?"

"No," Russ replied, with a chuckle. "Seven hundred donuts."

Chapter Seven

W hile Russ showered, Suzanne showed Jesse and Rusty to the rooms where they'd be staying, located in the north side of the house. Jesse could tell that the home had been enlarged at least once, and it looked like all the rooms on that side might've been one large addition.

"The room next door only has one bed," she said to Rusty. "So we thought you and Jesse's grandfather wouldn't mind sharing this one. It used to be my two brothers' room."

Jesse felt his face flush at the casual way she'd assumed he and Linda might be sleeping together.

"They move away?" Rusty asked, dropping his sea bag at the foot of one of the beds.

"My oldest brother, Jacob, was killed in Vietnam," she said. "And Billy, who is only a year older than me, lives in California."

"I'm sorry about your brother," Jesse said. "My dad was killed in Vietnam."

She glanced over at Jesse and gave him a somber nod of recognition.

"Anyway," she continued, "the only other option is a daybed in the nursery… with Russel Junior."

"This'll be fine," Rusty said, opening his sea bag and pulling the two shopping bags out. "We stopped and got ya somethin', and a toy for the little one."

"You didn't have to do that," she said, accepting the wine bottle with a smile. "But thank you. Russel loves having some of the guys out here on long weekends, and I enjoy playing hostess. Please consider this your home while you're here."

Jesse opened the door to the other room and put his seabag just inside, then turned back to Suzanne. "How old is your house?"

"That depends on which part you're in," she replied. "Come on. I'll show you around while Russel Junior's still asleep."

She led them back down the hall, explaining, "My grandfather added this whole side in 1924—three bedrooms and a bathroom. Russel uses the other bedroom on this side for sort of an office. He's getting more and more into looking for lost treasure, and as you saw, he has a knack for finding it."

They entered the living room again, which flowed into the dining room with polished hardwood floors. Just those two large rooms comprised most of the main living area.

Beyond the dining room, through a large archway, was a modern kitchen with windows above the sink looking out over the water, and a nine-pane glass door that opened onto the back deck.

"This used to be the whole house," Suzanne said, "not counting the kitchen back there."

Jesse measured the walls in his mind. "This couldn't have been more than five or six hundred square feet."

"The original house was built about 1730 and was just three rooms—the main room in front and two small bedrooms in back."

"From 1730 to 1924 is a long time for just two bedrooms," Jesse said. "Did your earlier ancestors not have many kids?"

"Some did," Suzanne replied. "Back then, bedrooms were just for sleeping, and there'd be four or five kids in one room. But Gramps and Gram had eight children. So, he built on that whole wing we just came from."

"Over two hundred years old," Rusty breathed. "That's older'n my folks' house."

"Back then, the kitchen was separate from the house because it was hot, and of course there was no plumbing, but there was an outhouse down by the water. The kitchen, two more bedrooms, and two more bathrooms were added in 1938, bringing it to its current 2,400 square feet, four times its original size. Russel and I just finished a complete remodeling last year, covering up and smoothing out the additions."

"You said the original house was built in 1730?" Rusty asked. "By William Howard?"

She nodded. "These planks are the original floor. Taken from the deck of his ship, *Revenge*."

"*Queen Anne's Revenge?*" Rusty asked.

"No, that sank down in Beaufort," she replied, her pronunciation indicating the city in North Carolina, not South Carolina. "William Howard gave his small sloop the name *Revenge* after he was pardoned and retired here."

"You're kiddin'!" Rusty replied, in obvious glee. "We're walkin' where pirates walked?"

"Well, he was retired by then," she said. "But maybe he had friends over. He lived to be 108."

Rusty laughed, perhaps a bit too loudly.

There was a squeal from the side of the house where they hadn't gone.

"He's awake!" she whisper-shouted with a smile. "Now's your chance to escape. Run while you can."

They both laughed as she hurried into the other wing of the house.

"Built in 1730," Rusty said softly. "By the second-in-command of ol' Edward Teach's crew. Ya know, at one time, he had five ships and over five hundred men."

"What's your obsession with pirates?" Jesse asked.

"I'm a Conch," Rusty replied matter-of-factly. "The Keys used to be a haven for pirates, buccaneers, wreckers, and bootleggers. My own great-grandpa was a bootlegger, and one or two of my ancestors' brothers or cousins mighta been wreckers."

Jesse noticed an area in the exposed-beam ceiling that was framed-in between two open rafters and pointed. "What do you think that is?"

Just then, Suzanne returned, holding the hand of a little boy, who was rubbing one eye with his knuckles.

"This is Russel Junior," she said. "And he has to eat *right now*, don't you, sweetheart?"

He had Russ's facial features, though a little plumper, but his mother's blond hair and blue eyes.

"Can you say hi to Jesse and Rusty?" she asked, leading him toward the kitchen.

He turned and waved. "Hi."

Then he climbed up into a highchair without any help and

Suzanne slid a tray in front of him, both to put his food on, and to secure the toddler in place.

She quickly got a jar of applesauce from the refrigerator and spooned some into a bowl, then placed it in front of the boy, along with a spoon.

"Have a seat," she said. "Can I get you anything? He can mostly feed himself now, but I have to be ready in case he drops his spoon."

"Thanks, we're good," Rusty said, as they sat down at the table with her. "Say, what's that framed-in part in the ceilin'?"

She glanced up in the living room. "Oh, that? It was originally built as an escape hatch."

"An escape hatch?" Jesse asked.

"In case of flooding when a hurricane comes," she replied. "If all else fails and the house is underwater, the roof is the highest place to be."

Jesse looked up at the opening and shuddered, knowing the most devastating part of a hurricane was the high surge of water that came ashore with it. Though he didn't remember it—he was only two at that time—he and his mother had survived Hurricane Isbell's 125 mile-per-hour winds at his grandparents' house, and he had heard the stories of the slashing wind and rain. But their house was ten miles from the coast.

He couldn't imagine the courage and desperation it would take to climb through that hole onto the open roof while a storm was raging all around, the whole island was inundated, and waves were rocking the foundation.

"The offshoot's awake," Russ said, entering the kitchen.

The boy smiled gleefully and jumped up and down in his seat.

"No, no," Russ said. "You're already a mess and I just got out of the shower. Finish eating, then Mom can clean you up."

Suzanne rose and kissed her husband. "You smell better now. Why don't y'all run down to the dock and show them the boat. I'll bring Russel Junior out when he's finished eating."

"Come on," Russ said, heading to the back door. "I think you guys'll like this."

They rose and followed him outside.

"We have some cold beer in the car," Rusty said, following Russ down the back steps to the patio.

"Go grab it," he replied. "We can add them to those in the fridge in the shop. But no heavy drinking, and last call's at midnight, ten hours before dive time."

"Why not dive earlier?" Jesse asked.

"We'll be diving deep," Russ explained. "Almost a hundred feet, so our bottom time is limited, and we'll make two dives, max—one at 1100 and the second at 1300. Visibility will be better just before and after noon. That'll give us two hours between dives."

"Sounds good to me," Rusty said. "Even with a two-hour surface interval, and maxin; our bottom time, a third dive that deep'd just be way over the limit."

Jesse followed Rusty, and they retrieved the cooler with the beer and rum from the car.

"What's this?" Russ asked, taking the bottle from Rusty. "Myers's?"

"Made from blackstrap molasses," Rusty said. "Way better'n Bacardi."

They went into the shop, removed the individual, stubby bottles of beer from the cooler, and placed them into the fridge.

"Jamaican beer?" Russ asked.

"Jamaican lager," Rusty said, handing him one. He looked up at Jesse. "You want one? It's beer-thirty."

Jesse nodded and accepted the bottle, then Rusty pulled an opener from his back pocket and passed it around.

Russ took a long pull on his bottle, then smacked his lips. "That *is* good. Red Stripe, huh?"

"And it ain't all that expensive," Rusty added. "If ya buy it in the Bahamas like my pop did. He brought over forty cases a few months back, and I been hangin' onto this last case for the right time."

The three of them went back outside and started walking leisurely down the long pier. Within a few steps, their footfalls became one.

"Shallow for a long way out?" Jesse asked.

"The pier's over two hundred feet long," Russ replied. "And only four feet deep at the end. From there, it's a winding cut to open water down near the inlet. And before you ask, this isn't the sandbar the battle was fought on."

"Sandbar?" Jesse asked.

"Both of Maynard's ships ran aground durin' the battle," Rusty began, "as well as both of Teach's, and it was a race to see who could float their boat first."

"From what most historians say," Russ added, pointing ahead, "it happened about half a mile beyond the end of my dock. The actual sandbar's gone now, rearranged by a few hurricanes since then."

Russ's boat was tied up alongside the end of the long dock, the bow pointing shoreward. It was big; easily thirty feet, and it had an enclosed wheelhouse with a wide-open deck behind it.

"*Dauntless* used to be a crab boat," Russ said. "Those guys go out in all kinds of weather and their boats are solid."

"You have radar?" Jesse asked, noting a unit on the roof.

"Sure do," Russ replied. "And it works. Like I said, those guys go out in anything."

"What's she got for power?" Rusty asked, measuring the boat with a practiced eye.

"An inboard Ford Lehman diesel," Russ replied. "A hundred and twenty horses. Easy on fuel and as reliable as they come. But slower than the speed of mud."

The cockpit had six scuba tanks secured under the gunwales on both sides, with an open dive bag and gear strewn all around the aft deck.

"I was just rinsing everything when I heard your car," Russ said, stepping down into the boat. "Already filled the tanks."

"You got fresh water all the way out here?" Rusty asked, eyeing a hose bib mounted on the dock.

"I ran a pipe under the pier from the cistern a few years ago. It hasn't been used in decades but was once the only water source for the house. Come on aboard."

Rusty stepped down into the boat first and looked toward the open water of the sound. "She don't hardly roll at all."

"Crab boats are mostly flat-bottomed at the stern," Russ said, as Jesse joined them. "Stable in calm water at the docks for unloading, but rolly as hell out in the sound when pulling traps."

"How far offshore will we be goin'?" Rusty asked, turning around.

"Eighteen miles from the inlet," Russ replied. "About eight miles off Cape Hatteras."

Jesse looked into the wheelhouse. There was a small hatch to the left of the wheel, which was slightly right of center.

"There's a cabin?" he asked.

"Small one," Russ replied. "A sink and two bunks, plus a little storage. The foot of one bunk is beside the engine, and the foot of the upper is under the helm."

On the dash, in front of the wheel, was a typical radio and compass, along with all the usual engine gauges, plus a black box with a small display of some kind.

He stepped into the wheelhouse. "What's this?"

Russ looked up, then followed him inside. "That's a game-changer," he replied, a note of pride in his voice. "Not just for treasure hunting, but for diving, fishing and crabbing, too. Maybe even for everyday boaters one day."

"What is it?" Rusty asked, examining the front.

"That's what's going to get us to the exact spot, eighteen miles from here," Russ replied. "It's a Walker Marine Sat-Nav 802. With it, I can find any given location, within about a hundred feet."

"Sat-nav?" Jesse asked. "Satellite navigation?"

Russ waved a hand across the sky. "NASA's been putting satellites up there for years, and they don't do anything but allow a receiver like this to pick up radio waves from several of them, to triangulate its position."

"Pop was tellin' me about this," Rusty said. "But I thought it was mostly just for military and big ships."

"It was," Russ said with a nod, switching the unit on. "Until a couple of years ago."

Jesse could hear the quiet hum of a cooling fan, plus a series of random clicks. After a moment, a string of numbers appeared on the little display.

Rusty leaned closer. "Is that our latitude and longitude?"

"Accurate to within one second of arc at the equator," Russ replied.

Rusty whistled softly. "That exact, huh?"

"One second of arc?" Jesse asked. "Like in degrees, minutes, and seconds? How far is that?"

Russ and Rusty turned to him and said at the same time, "A hundred feet."

Chapter Eight

❖━━━❖━━━❖━━━❖━━━❖

Though the weather was cool, the sun had been beating down on the boat's occupants all day long, and at the slow speed they'd been forced to travel, it had become quite hot in the uncovered helm and cockpit area, and it'd been a long and boring day.

But it would soon be over, and the end of the day would be a roar of loud racing engines and excitement, not to mention a six-figure payday.

The freighter was getting closer to the Outer Banks of North Carolina, and they'd be taking off soon.

Ringo sat at the wheel as the boat idled along on just one engine. After getting the call from the ship's captain the night before, advising him when the cargo ship would be passing Wrightsville Beach, he'd put together the needed supplies for the trip, gotten a little sleep, and locked up the house well before dawn.

To say that Ringo Thomas was an impatient man would be

an understatement. He wasn't happy unless he was going a hundred miles an hour with his hair on fire. But he knew the payoff at the end of the haul would be worth the torment he was putting his engines through.

The cost of doing business, he thought. All businesses had overhead, and his had double overhead—as in the valves of each engine's heads.

But now, he had a line on a replacement boat that might suit his needs to get out of the business, and he was excited to see it later that evening.

Roy had called back and said everything was set for the day after tomorrow, but they could go down to the marina in the morning to give it a once-over ahead of the sea trial.

He was excited, but in a different way. He'd have to force himself to alter and slow his lifestyle.

The engines the Cigarette 41 came with were great for cruising around and casual racing, but his were better. They were built for racing, covering great distances in the open ocean at high speed, not puttering along on one engine until it started to overheat, then switching to the other. They just couldn't get enough cool seawater when running at an idle for too long.

And they sucked an awful lot of gas. Not idling like they were—the gas gauge had hardly moved off full all day. But very soon, he'd make a high-speed run from the ocean into Pamlico Sound to meet a truck on the mainland. It was a total of about sixty miles, and the engines would burn through more than a hundred gallons of high-octane. They'd have to gas up before heading back to Wilmington, but there were lots of marinas on the mainland where they didn't ask questions if you paid in cash.

He hoped his next boat would be able to eat up mile after

mile at their current speed, sipping just a little fuel, and traveling hundreds or even thousands of miles without stopping.

He'd thought about a sailboat. That'd be the farthest removed from his business and lifestyle, but sailing seemed complicated. He'd always been a "turn the keys and point the bow" kind of guy.

Moose sat in back, constantly moving the load around, changing and rearranging the bricks of cocaine. He'd have to leave them alone once they got moving.

They'd already made the exchange with the freighter captain, cash for cocaine, with armed men standing over them and watching every move. Now, they were just waiting until they had a little more distance from a Coast Guard boat that'd been stationed off Cape Lookout, twenty-five miles to the southwest.

The patrol boat had come out as the freighter passed, and Ringo had to rely on the captain to let him know where the patrol boat was, so Ringo could keep the large freighter between them.

If they'd decided to stop and search the freighter, Ringo's boat would be spotted, exposing the cargo vessel for what it was, resulting in even closer scrutiny.

Their plan, if it ever looked like that was going to happen, was to haul ass away from the ship, using it to block the Coast Guard's eyes and radar, until they were far enough away to not be visible—at least five miles.

The patrol boat had finally headed back toward the cape after nearly circling the freighter at a distance.

"How much longer, man?" Tim asked. "We got the shit, we know where the truck's gonna be. Sittin' out here is dangerous."

"We wait until the coast is clear," Ringo replied. "That's an old pirate's term and it means exactly that. We can't be seen leaving this ship. He's got a powerful radar. What do we have? A compass."

He'd known Tim for most of his life. The two had grown up in the same area, gone to the same schools, and ran with the same bunch of people as teens and young adults. Tim was a better-than-average mechanic and actually knew a thing or two about boats as well.

"I'm gonna lay down," Moose said, passing between the two front seats and starting down into the boat's interior.

Ringo let him go. Moose knew the cabin was bare of everything except a commode and the raised platform in front that once had a mattress on it.

The walkie-talkie on the dash crackled and Ringo picked it up, pulling the antenna all the way out. It was what he and the captain had communicated with, even when the Coast Guard patrol boat was nearby—a kid's toy that could barely reach across a backyard.

He started the port engine and put it in gear, bumping both engines up in speed, just a little over an idle. He was hoping it was the call he'd been waiting for, but he'd have to move to within a football field to pick up the captain's walkie-talkie.

When he was in range, he held the toy radio to his mouth, the antenna sticking up above his head. "Was that you, Tony?"

The radio crackled again and then the captain's voice came on. "I see nothing on radar for thirty miles. Time to earn your money. Make your heading two-seven-five degrees to the inlet, fifteen miles."

"Roger that," Ringo said, then pushed the antenna down and dropped the walkie-talkie in a pouch on the side of the seat.

"Time to go?" Tim asked.

"Yeah, get Moose up," Ringo replied. "I'll need him to help balance the boat."

Ringo looked over his shoulder at the pile of plastic-wrapped bricks of coke, stacked unevenly on the floor in front of the backseats, each measuring about eight inches square and twelve long. Twenty individually wrapped five-kilo bricks of nose candy made for an easy-to-move ballast.

Moose was six-five and easily weighed three hundred pounds, so his nickname fit. He was mostly muscle… and had a thick head. Once they got moving, he'd have to shift the bricks around, or even his own body, to help balance the load.

"I ain't feelin' so good," the big man said, struggling to get through the companionway. "All this rockin' and rollin'. And did you know there's some kinda gremlin or something down there?"

"Just get back there in the middle seat," Ringo said, turning the boat toward the stern of the freighter. "You might only need to lean one way or the other, and the wind in your face will help."

Moose had a lot of purposes, all requiring his huge size and strength, but when it came to brain power, he was a few cards short of a full deck, and the deck was loaded with jokers. He'd been in and out of a number of mental institutions. He wasn't crazy, he just wasn't smart, and at his size, that scared people. Moose often made poor decisions if left on his own, and most of those poor decisions involved women.

The trim tabs would do the job of leveling the boat, but during a high-speed run across flat, shallow water, they created undue drag, bogging the boat down. But having Moose in back with the cargo meant he could move a brick here or there and get the boat perfectly balanced with the trim tabs in the neutral position.

Moose climbed into the back and situated himself in the middle seat, strapping just the lap belt on to allow himself to bend and move bricks around. This wasn't his first rodeo either.

Tim took his seat on the left side and like Ringo, buckled both the lap belt as well as the two shoulder belts as he studied the gauges.

"Our heading will be two-seven-five," Ringo told him. "We're fifteen miles from the inlet and I'll run at sixty, so we should see the markers after twelve minutes or so."

"The right engine's a little hot," Tim said, "but not too bad. It should cool down once we get movin'. The left one's just gettin' into the warm range. Oil pressure's good on both, and the batteries are chargin'."

"Turn on the sat-nav and put in the numbers for the middle one, Ocracoke Inlet."

They continued to idle due west, using the compass on the dash as the cargo ship continued north. After a moment, the ship had moved out of their way and Tim had the satellite navigation machine working.

"Looks like you're almost on the right course," he said. "This says the same thing—275 degrees at sixty miles per hour, and we should be in the inlet in fifteen minutes."

"We'll look for the markers in twelve or thirteen," Ringo said. "I know one of my companies sells electronics, but I still trust my eyes more. Ready?"

"Let 'em rip!" Tim replied, as Moose grunted something in the affirmative.

"Okay," Ringo shouted, reaching for the throttles. "Hang on!"

He brought the speed up slowly, so as not to launch the boat out of the water. Once they reached twenty miles per hour with the boat planing nicely, he increased speed until the big round speedometer hit 60, then pulled back a little to maintain that speed.

In the back, Moose shoved a couple of bricks to the left side of the boat, looked up at the horizon through the windshield, then moved one more just a few inches to the left and a third forward as far as he could reach.

It looked like a haphazardly piled bunch of bricks of coke, but in Moose's mind, everything was right where it was supposed to be.

The guy might not understand a whole lot, Ringo thought. But when it came to balancing a load on a boat, Moose just had a knack.

The ocean was fairly calm, as calm as it ever got in that area, and the wind and waves were behind them as the boat launched over the small rollers with ease, barely coming out of the water, then settling back in with a slight thud and a blast of spray from just behind the midpoint of the boat. Exactly what it was made to do.

Any faster and he'd surely have to saw the throttles back and forth each time the props came out of the water to prevent over-revving the engines.

In twelve minutes, the coast became visible as the sun neared the horizon far to the left of the bow. Half a minute later, Tim pointed.

"Red marker! Dead ahead!"

"I don't see it yet!" Ringo shouted over the engine, wind, and waves.

Tim leaned forward, studying the numbers on the display. One string showed where they were, and another showed where they were going.

"Come due west!" Tim shouted. "Put that marker to starboard when you see it. We're on the exact same latitude as the inlet."

Ringo adjusted their course slightly, holding the mark on the compass as close to the center of the W as he could.

Tim rose as much as the seatbelts would allow, taking the full wind in his face. Ringo could actually feel the change in the boat's handling from the increased wind drag on one side.

"There!" Tim shouted. "Just a hair to the right! See where there ain't no surf? That's the inlet!"

A moment later, they tore through the opening in the barrier islands and entered Pamlico Sound, no other boats in sight.

The patrol boat never spotted us, Ringo thought, reading the shallow water ahead.

"Wait until we clear the shoal!" Tim shouted. "I'm puttin' the numbers in for the pickup spot! But it's sure to be northwest after the shallows!"

"There's people on the dock over to the right!" Moose shouted from behind. "They need a bigger boat!"

Ringo glanced over, spotting an old crab boat with several men and a beautiful blonde on board, standing at the stern with a little boy.

"Just some crabbers!" he yelled back to the big man. "They can't do anything to us!"

He looked quickly at the woman on the boat again and smiled sadistically. "Oh, but what I could do to that," he mumbled.

Chapter Nine

————◆————◆————◆————◆————

Jesse and Rusty helped Russ in rinsing and hanging his dive gear and when they finished, they sat on the gunwales and watched as the sun got closer to the waters of Pamlico Sound. The mainland was that way, but far over the horizon and completely out of sight. There still wasn't a cloud visible anywhere. Just the sky and the water.

"This is my favorite time of day," Suzanne said, as she and the boy reached the boat.

They were both barefoot and she carried a metal bucket.

"You all cleaned up, little man?" Russ asked, moving to help his son into the boat.

Russ picked him up and held him with one arm as he took his wife's hand with the other so she could step down.

"He ate all his applesauce and a whole bunch of grapes," she said, then turned and handed Rusty the pail. "I brought a few more of your Jamaican beers."

Russ put the boy down on the deck and he went straight to the stern, where the transom was at chin-height for him, and

71

looked out toward the setting sun, its rays dancing across the water.

Rusty pulled his opener from his pocket, quickly opened the four bottles and passed them around.

"Sunset is a time for reflection," Suzanne said, leaning on the transom beside her son. "A time to think about everything you accomplished that day, and how you might do better tomorrow."

"My pap... er, grandfather, says the same thing," Jesse offered.

"How long you had that sat-nav thing?" Rusty asked.

"I got it several months ago," Russ replied. "But I haven't had a lot of time to use it until I went on leave last week. You watch and see. In the morning, we'll head out to where I found those coins and that necklace and continue searching the exact spot I found them."

"If it's only accurate to a hundred feet," Jesse began, "won't it be hard to find the *exact* spot? A hundred-foot circle is over thirty *thousand* square feet of surface area—three quarters of an acre."

"You do that in your head?" Russ asked quizzically.

Rusty laughed. "He does it all the time. The man's a walkin' addin' machine."

"You're right, Jesse," Russ said. "Finding the *precise* spot would be impossible with the short bottom time we'll have. So, when I finished my dives today, I left a weighted float. The float's small and white, and twenty feet below the surface. We'll go to the latitude and longitude I have written down and just look around till we see the float."

"Then just drop the anchor right there?" Rusty asked. "How

much anchor rode you got on this boat?"

"A hundred feet of chain and four hundred feet of three-eighth-inch braided nylon. It's been pretty calm the last few days, though. So I don't see why we can't all dive at once."

"And leave the boat unattended?" Suzanne asked.

"I've been diving it solo for several days, and you came out with me that one day. Did you see any other boats?"

"Not seeing them doesn't mean one isn't there," she replied. "No boat would be visible outside of a few miles."

"The radar has a twenty-four-mile range, babe," he said. "And we'll check it often and before each dive."

Far in the distance, Jesse could hear a low growling sound that he at first thought was the surf getting bigger on the other side of the island.

The others heard it, too, and Suzanne moved to the transom and stood beside her son.

"That's an engine," Rusty said, turning toward the sound.

"Two engines," Russ muttered, just as a long, sleek boat came into view, flying through the inlet.

The sound of the engines grew louder as the dark blue boat sped away from the narrow opening just a few hundred yards away. The hull almost melded with the dark grays and greens of the background in the dwindling daylight. The white water it churned gave it away as it sped across the water at what Jesse figured had to be at least fifty or sixty miles per hour.

Two men rode in front, and a third, who was either standing up, or was unusually tall, rode in back. He turned and pointed a long arm at them.

"Damned drug runners," Russ growled.

"Drug runners?" Jesse asked. "Here?"

"They go out to meet cargo ships," Russ said. "At least that's what everyone around here figures. Cocaine smugglers, using boats that are so fast, the Coast Guard can't even track them."

"But why here?" Jesse persisted. "This is just a string of little islands with a handful of small towns."

"The drugs aren't for here," Suzanne said. "That boat will meet a truck somewhere on the mainland, to carry the drugs to Raleigh or Charlotte or somewhere else."

"This is a good place for them to do it because of the dangerous sandbars," Russ added, his hardened features locked on the fast-moving boat. "Look. With only a foot in the water, he's flying right across the sandbar."

"We see those a lot in the Keys," Rusty said, an obvious note of disdain in his voice. "Especially up around Miami. We call 'em cocaine cowboys."

"Can't the police do anything?" Jesse asked. "Follow them on radar or something?"

Russ nodded. "The Coasties do. Right up until they reach one of the three inlets. Coast Guard boats are slower and have to navigate the cuts. The little bay boats used by the sheriff could never catch those things, and none of those have radar. By the time the Coast Guard gets inside the sound to relay the location, the drug runners are gone."

Jesse looked over at Russ. "How fast are they?"

"I've seen 'em doin' over eighty," Rusty said. "Same kinda boat, just without all the 'creature comforts.' That boat was doin' sixty, and from the sound of them engines, he still had a lot of pedal to go."

"But if there's only three inlets," Jesse said, "can't they just blockade them when the drug boats go out?"

"That's just it," Russ said. "There aren't any boats like that around here. We think they shadow the freighters, staying out of sight until they make the run for shore. No telling where they come from."

As the boat disappeared from sight, they could still hear it. The sun reached the horizon and seemed to rest on it for a moment, then it slowly dipped below the surface and was gone.

"When is your grandfather arriving?" Suzanne asked. "Russel told me he's a Marine also."

"Late tomorrow evening," Jesse replied. "And yeah, he served in the Pacific. I sure do appreciate your hospitality on short notice."

"He's a World War II vet," Russ said. "We're honored."

"Well, I'm grateful, just the same," Jesse said. "I was feeling guilty about not telling him I was taking leave and not coming to see him and Mam. This will be my first birthday away from home."

"It's your birthday?" Suzanne asked with excitement.

Jesse nodded. "On Thursday. But he's only staying until Monday."

She turned to her husband. "We'll all go to Howard's Pub tomorrow night to celebrate. I'll get Natalie to babysit."

"Great idea!" Russ said. "You haven't been out of the house in ten days."

"You don't have to make a big deal," Jesse said, feeling awkward.

"Forget it," Russ said. "I promise you'll earn your keep."

The boy, who'd been standing with his hands on the boat's transom, turned around. "More, Dada."

Russ laughed. "Oh no, little man. One sunset a day. If I do more all the time, it won't be magic."

"The bugs'll be out soon," Suzanne said. "I'm going to get him back up to the house and get dinner started. The potatoes will take an hour and you need to light the grill."

Russ looked at his wristwatch. "Synchronize for 1930?"

"That'll be perfect," she replied.

"We'll be up in a few minutes," he said, hugging her, then lifting his son up to the dock.

Suzanne took his hand. "Say goodbye, Russel, Junior."

"Bye," the boy said, then turned and started up the dock with Suzanne following him.

"That boy cracks me up," Russ said. "I never thought I'd be much of a father, but we dads have the easy job—playing with them and keeping them active and in line. Pretty much like I do you knuckleheads."

"Do you always call him Russel Junior?" Rusty asked, looking after the boy as he continued up the dock. "Why not call him just Junior? Half as many syllables. Or even JR."

"We've thought about it," Russ said. "Suze wants to wait a while before we stick a nickname on him that he might carry the rest of his life."

"Yeah," Jesse agreed. "And what if he passes the name on to *his* son one day. They can't both be Junior."

"Deuce," Rusty suggested with a grin. "That'd make you Ace."

Russ looked at him for a second. "Deuce, huh?"

"Me and my girl, Jewels, wanna have kids as soon as we get married."

"When will that be?" Russ asked, leaning on the gunwale in thought.

"End of next year," Rusty replied. "Or sooner, if I pick up corporal."

"Then you should figure on sooner," Russ said. "I'd be really surprised if both you guys aren't NCOs by this time next year. What about you, Jesse? I know you and Walkley have been seeing each other. No girl back home?"

"There was one once," Jesse replied. "But no, nobody at home waiting for me."

"Well, watch yourself on Court Street," he said. "There are a lot of local girls and Japanese ex-wives down there, looking to land another jarhead."

Jesse glanced once more in the direction where the racing boat had gone. "He'll have to come back out, right?"

"The drug runner?" Russ asked. "Yeah, probably late tonight. But by then the boat'll be empty, and the law can't do anything. Had one fly right past my boat once. If I'd had a thumper, he'd have been toast."

By "thumper," Jesse knew Russ was referring to the M-209 grenade launcher that could be attached below the handgrip and barrel of an M-16 rifle.

"Careful," Rusty said. "With today's politics, just thinkin' that could bring a shitstorm down on ya."

Russ grinned. "In the 'Old Corps' we didn't care much about someone getting their feelings hurt." He nodded his chin in the direction in which the boat had disappeared. "If some scum like that disappeared, nobody would care. People involved in that shit chose their path a long time ago, and thus, their demise. Karma can be a bitch sometimes."

Chapter Ten

———◆———◆———◆———◆———

Jesse carefully considered what Russ had said. He'd often felt the same way. Just three months earlier, a man had died by his hand. He'd allowed a cop to take the blame and himself the permission to let it go, because he knew that sooner or later, the guy who'd called himself Sideshift Brisco would have run up against the law or someone else who was bigger, stronger, faster, or better armed. In the end, it'd been Brisco who'd been better armed, but he'd wrongly assumed that because of his size, he didn't need the gun.

"You really think we'll find somethin'?" Rusty asked.

"I'd almost bet on it," Russ replied. "I had two more hits on my metal detector just as I was about to surface."

"You got an underwater detector?" Rusty asked incredulously. "I thought that was like Buck Rogers shit."

"They're pretty new on the market," Russ admitted. "A company in Germany started mass production last year."

"Can't be cheap."

Russ chuckled. "I know. How's a grunt sergeant afford it? Well, my hobby fuels my investment in it. I'll sell those gold coins from earlier this week, plus the silver coins from today. We'll bank that until I get back from Japan, and then I might buy a bigger boat."

"That's how Pap built his business," Jesse said. "After the war, he and Mam lived frugally, and he put everything back into his business, hiring the best people he could find and expanding."

Russ arched an eyebrow. "You said he was an architect? What's his business worth now?"

"He sold it nine years ago," Jesse replied. "When I went to live with them."

Russ arched an eyebrow. "Sounds like your grandparents took over the parenting duties pretty seriously."

Jesse nodded. "I suppose they did. I never considered all the sacrifices they made until recently."

When they returned to the house, Suzanne was busy setting the outside table on the deck, complete with a heavy tablecloth, silverware, porcelain china, wine and water glasses, and linen napkins.

She truly seemed happy being wife, mother, and hostess, and Jesse couldn't help thinking that Gina wasn't the type to be able to fill those roles. If that was even what he wanted in a wife. He just wasn't sure. But Russ and Suzanne seemed happy.

Still, it was a blow to his ego when Gina left.

Russ opened the grill and started scrubbing the grates with a large wire brush. Then he pointed to a heavy-looking wooden chest under the porch. "There's a bucket in there. Would one of you fill it and bring it over?"

Jesse opened the chest to find it had a watertight seal around the top and a large metal bucket inside. The bucket rested on top of a pile of large wood chunks, some as big as his fist, that looked like they'd already been burned. He filled the bucket, careful not to get any soot on his hands.

Russ was removing the cast iron grates when Jesse brought the bucket of burned wood chunks over.

"Just dump it right in there with what was left from the last cook," Russ said. "That's kiln-dried oak, and that little bit will burn for hours."

He spread the wood around with a small shovel, leaving a depression in the middle. Then he squirted just a little lighter fluid in the center, and after a moment, dropped a lit match in.

Blue flames danced around the middle of the grill for a moment before Russ covered them with chunks from the sides, put the grates back in place, and lowered the hood.

He adjusted the damper and flue, then turned around. "That'll take about ten or fifteen minutes to get up to the right temperature. How about we try that molasses rum?"

"Shot glasses or highball and mixers?" Suzanne asked, leaning over the rail.

"No, ma'am," Rusty called up. "I mean, this is a sippin' rum. Rocks glasses, or lowball, if ya got 'em?"

She smiled and gave him a thumbs-up. "I have just the thing."

"How is it you know about rocks glasses and rums?" Russ asked.

"Pop runs a bar and bait shop back home," Rusty replied. "I been tendin' bar since I was fourteen or so."

Where'd you leave it?" Jesse asked Rusty. "The rum, I mean."

"In the fridge with the beer," he replied with a grin. "Like I said, it's a sippin' rum… best served cold."

Russ grinned. "Just like revenge."

Rusty trotted toward the shop by the pier and returned a moment later carrying the dark brown bottle with its distinctive yellow label.

Suzanne came down the steps with a wine glass in one hand, along with the bottle Rusty and Jesse had given her, and in the other, she had three small drink glasses pinched between her thumb and fingers.

Rusty took the glasses from her and set them on a small table, then opened the rum.

"I think I'll stick with the grapes," Suzanne said, handing Jesse the bottle, then a corkscrew she pulled from her pocket. "Will you do the honors, Jesse?"

Jesse had only opened a wine bottle a couple of times in his whole life, and after peeling the label off, he clumsily screwed the tip of the screw into the top of the cork. Gripping the bottle low in his left hand, he pulled the cork out with his right, then offered to pour it for her.

Suzanne raised a hand up, stopping him when the glass was less than half full. "That's enough. Someone besides Russel Junior has to stay sober."

Russ looked at a small gauge in the grill's hood, and, judging it hot enough, he opened it and began scrubbing the now-heated grates with the wire brush. Without looking back at her, he asked, "What do you think of Deuce, Suze?"

"Deuce what?" she asked, then took a small sip of wine.

"Russel Junior," he replied. "Russel the second... Deuce?"

She looked over at the boy, who was pushing a big Tonka dump truck around in the sandbox.

"Deuce," she whispered, as if tasting the word on her tongue. "Then if there's a third, he could be Trey?"

"What would the fourth be?" Jesse asked, then swallowed a small sip of the rum.

Russ chuckled. "By the time that boy becomes a grandpa, I'll be long dead. Not my circus, not my monkeys."

"I like it," she said, then turned and smiled at her husband. "And you'll be Ace."

"Think it'll confuse him?" Russ asked. "If we start calling him something else?"

"Let's think about it a little more," she said. "I'll go get the steaks."

"It's gotta be rough," Rusty said, once she'd gone inside. "I mean, you bein' over in Oki a whole year and her all alone with the boy. I been home twice in the last six months and I miss Jewels somethin' fierce."

"Suze is the most independent woman you'll ever find," Russ said. "We've been through this twice already; Vietnam and my first tour in Oki."

"They'll stay in Jacksonville?" Jesse asked.

Russ shook his head. "We'll close up the Tarawa Terrace house, like before. She's got a lot of family here on the island and dozens of cousins all up and down the OBX." He paused and glanced up at the house. "It'll be harder for me."

Then he turned and faced Rusty. "If you and your girl are set on getting married, you should wait until after."

Rusty looked puzzled. "After what?"

"You'll likely get orders to Japan yourself," he said. "Most of infantry spend a year overseas in their first enlistment."

"Okinawa?"

"Most likely," Russ replied, as the door up on the deck opened and closed. "Or the Mideast. That civil war in Lebanon is still going on, and there's rumors we might get involved at some point."

Jesse hadn't thought much about being deployed, but he knew it was a part of the job. Most infantry Marines deployed twice in their first enlistment, and there'd been a lot of saber-rattling going on in places like Lebanon and Ethiopia, not to mention the full-scale war with the Soviets in Afghanistan.

Marines trained daily for combat in whatever terrain or climate they might be sent to.

"This is good," Russ said, taking another sip of his rum. "Thanks."

"Thanks for havin' us," Rusty said, as Suzanne came down the steps with a big platter covered by four large steaks.

She placed it on the small table beside the grill, then turned toward Russ. "Can I have a sip?"

He handed her his glass. "It's pretty strong."

She took a small taste, barely wetting her lips, then her face screwed up like she'd bitten into a lime.

"It's burny," she said, smacking her lips. "But it has a flavor... kind of tropical."

"That'd be the blackstrap molasses, allspice, and pineapple," Rusty said. "Some can taste a hint of coffee and leather, but I don't know 'bout that."

Russ opened the hood on the grill, and Jesse noted that the

small fire had spread throughout the grill's pit, more smoldering embers than flame.

One by one, Russ put the steaks on, each one sizzling on contact with the cast iron grates, then he closed the hood. "How long for the potatoes?"

"About twenty or twenty-five minutes," she replied.

He reached under the grill and partly closed the dampers, then did the same thing with the flue. "Two turns," he said, looking at his watch. "Five minutes on each side, then rest for five."

"Do you grill a lot?" Jesse asked.

"Every night we're out here," Suzanne replied. "I do all the cooking at our home in Tarawa Terrace." Then she looked up at Jesse. "How old will you be on Thursday?"

"Eighteen," he replied.

She continued looking at him for a moment. "I don't believe you."

"It's true," Rusty said. "He cut the cake at the birthday ball with the battalion sergeant major. Remember?"

She smiled. "Yes, I do. And you danced with Gray Redmond's adorable little girl, Maggie."

Jesse nodded, remembering the cake-cutting ceremony, and meeting a lot of NCOs, staff NCOs, officers, and their wives and families. As the youngest and oldest Marines in the battalion, he and Sergeant Major Montoya had cut and served the first two slices of the birthday cake to each other, using the sergeant major's NCO sword.

"I enlisted right after my seventeenth birthday," Jesse said, "and shipped to Parris Island two months later, just three days after graduating high school."

"That's awfully young," she said. "Do you think you were ready for the 'Big Green Machine' at that age?"

Jesse looked down at her, a serious expression on his face. "I'd been planning on it since I skipped a grade in school when I was nine."

Chapter Eleven

---◆---◆---◆---◆---◆---

Russ had seared the steaks to perfection, and the vegetables had been grown in Suzanne's own garden on the corner of the property. Even Russel Junior enjoyed several small bites of Suzanne's steak.

Once they finished the meal, Suzanne took the toddler upstairs for his bath and put him to bed, while Jesse and Rusty pitched in to help Russ with the dishes.

The three of them worked quietly and efficiently, falling into a routine, with Jesse doing the washing, Rusty drying, and Russ putting everything away.

With the chore out of the way in less than ten minutes, they returned to the lower patio and pulled a pair of outdoor chairs and a small couch closer to the grill for warmth.

Though Russ had closed the dampers and flue, suffocating the fire, the coals in the grill were still hot, causing the metal to tick occasionally as it cooled in the chilly night air.

Jesse and Rusty sat in the two chairs, while Russ plopped down on the couch and pulled three cigars from his shirt pocket.

"The smoking lamp is lit, gentlemen."

"Whatcha got there?" Rusty asked, leaning toward him.

"Cuban contraband," Russ replied with a grin. "A buddy of mine who works in supply down in Gitmo sent me a whole box."

Rusty took one. "Thanks. Cuba's less'n a hundred miles from where I live, and a good friend of mine's dad is a cigar roller."

Russ offered one to Jesse, who took it. He didn't like cigars, or even cigarettes; they made him dizzy and nauseous. But he didn't want to offend the man he'd come to see as a mentor and friend.

Russ produced a Zippo lighter and lit his, puffing on the cigar, then passed the lighter around. Jesse's cigar was already clipped and punched, so he watched the other two.

Rusty lit his and puffed it to get it going. "Ya really think we might go to Lebanon?"

He handed the Zippo to Jesse, who lit his cigar, puffing on it like the other two had done. The taste of the smoke was strong, and Jesse avoided inhaling it.

"Lebanon's civil war—a *religious* war—has been going on for five years," Russ replied, blowing a blue-gray cloud of smoke into the night sky. "I don't see it ending any time soon. Not with the Iranian revolution last year."

"How so?" Jesse asked, almost coughing.

"Look, if you just erase the borders," Russ explained, "and leave the different religious sects, factions, and tribes all over the Mideast, you'll see that the region as a whole hasn't known peace in all of recorded history. Adding all those imaginary lines, it's just a matter of time before other nations get sucked in, because it's not about the lines."

"I'm just a boot grunt," Jesse said. "All I know is what I've seen on TV and learned in school. How is what's happening in Lebanon a threat to *our* national security?"

"Oil," Rusty said. "Whoever controls the oil controls the world economy."

Russ pointed his cigar at him. "Bingo."

"But Lebanon doesn't produce any oil," Jesse said. "So why would it be so important?"

"Religious numbers," Russ replied. "Like I said, erase the borders and look at the sects. There are Suni Muslims in almost all the Mideast countries. Same with the Shia. The biggest sect controls the whole region, and religion rules those countries. Old Brezhnev thought he could expand the Soviet empire into the region with ease, but they've been bogged down in Afghanistan for a decade now. Mark my words, they'll give up and pull out of there. Soviet troops are almost all conscripted, and they can't handle the terrain or the determination of the Afghan people."

Rusty nodded. "By addin' the people of Lebanon who are the same religious sect, they become stronger."

"Right again," Russ said. "Strength in numbers."

The door to the deck opened, and a moment later, Suzanne entered the small circle of light at the foot of the steps.

"He's asleep," she said. "I hope the meat doesn't upset his tummy."

Russ chuckled. "The boy's a carnivore, Suze."

"What time are you heading out in the morning?" she asked. "I packed enough food for a full day and then some."

"Same as today," he replied. "Sleep in, pull away from the dock at zero-eight, dive a couple of hours around noon, then back to the dock by early evening." He took her hand and pulled her down onto the couch with him. "So don't call the Coasties until after dark."

"Oh, I don't worry," she said. "I just like to know, so I can plan."

"How's this underwater detector work?" Rusty asked. "Is it like the ones you use on land?"

"Similar," Russ replied. "Same principle, but since you're underwater and horizontal, they're not nearly as long or heavy."

"Accurate?" Jesse asked.

"Very," he replied. "It can tell the difference between gold, silver, or an iron cannonball, up to three feet below the sand."

"Three feet?" Jesse asked.

"It's not like on shore," Russ replied, "where you might have denser rocks just below the surface. Out there, it's just sand; and the bottom is constantly scoured by the Gulf Stream."

Rusty looked over at him, concern in his eyes. "We're gonna anchor in a hundred feet, in the Stream, with a short rode?"

"The Stream is actually just beyond Diamond Shoal, but there's a feeder eddy on the inside, between the two shoals. That's where we'll be diving."

"Strong current?" Rusty asked.

"She'll hold," Russ replied, with a grin. "You didn't notice the ground tackle?"

Rusty shook his head.

Russ puffed on his cigar, now half gone. "Seventy-pound Fortress aluminum anchor. The Gulf Stream only flows at three knots here and this eddy runs about one or two."

"On that little boat?" Rusty asked, then nodded in agreement. "With a hundred feet of chain and a five-to-one scope?

Yeah, I'd say that'd hold ya in a good *four- to five*-knot current pretty good. I'd like more rode, but it'd just be a longer swim."

"Besides," Jesse added, "even if the anchor line parted, with only fifteen minutes of bottom time, the boat would only drift half a mile by the time we surfaced."

Russ chuckled. "And since you're the better swimmer, I'll hold your gear while you go get my boat."

They all laughed, until suddenly Jesse heard the sound of the racing boat's engines far to the north, moving across the water at high speed.

"Sounds like that boat's coming back," he said, rising and looking out over the water, though it was much too dark to see.

They listened for several minutes, then Russ said, "It doesn't sound like it's headed back this way."

"Is there another inlet to the north?" Rusty asked, also standing up.

"Hatteras Inlet is just seventeen miles up the coast," Suzanne told them, as she and Russ joined them at the edge of the patio. "And Oregon Inlet is more than forty miles past that, closer to the mainland."

The sound of the engines dropped in pitch.

"Hatteras," Russ said. "We'd never hear it from way up at Oregon Inlet. Besides, the bridge there makes it difficult at idle speed."

"It stopped," Jesse said, listening more intently. "Why would they stop? Is that inlet smaller?"

"Wider," Russ replied. "But not as easy to navigate as here. So maybe they just slowed down."

The three of them waited, listening for the sound of the

engines to ramp back up as the boat headed back out into the ocean.

It didn't.

Chapter Twelve

---◆---◆---◆---◆---

Dawn broke, with the sky looking much as it had the day before, bright and sunny, with just a handful of puffy white clouds off to the south. The temperature was a bit cooler than the previous morning, but Jesse and Rusty had awakened a hundred miles farther south and well inland.

Suzanne prepared eggs, bacon, and toast, and after a quick breakfast with Russel Junior, they headed down to the dock, Jesse and Rusty both carrying their dive bags.

"Y'all be careful," Suzanne said, as Russ stepped aboard.

"We'll be back before 1600," he reminded her, then inserted the key and started the engine. "Hopefully with some more trinkets."

The diesel engine burbled softly; the exhaust was dampened by the water flowing out with it.

Rusty and Jesse untied the dock lines, then Russ shifted to reverse, just as Rusty pushed the stern away from the pier.

"And we're off," Russ declared. "With any luck, you two will return to the base with a little more coin in your pockets than you left with."

"You're that sure, huh?" Rusty asked. "I mean, it's one big-ass ocean out there."

As the boat backed away, Russ turned on the radio and switched the channel to a monotonous voice giving the weather forecast for later in the week.

He looked at Rusty and held up one finger. "We find just one guinea, no matter who finds it, you two get paid $175 each tonight. A guy called me this morning and offered seven hundred each for as many as I had. He'll stop by this evening around 1800."

Russ put the boat in forward as he turned the wheel a full revolution, then brought the engine RPMs up a little. The boat's stern kicked around, and he straightened the wheel, heading almost due south.

"Jump up front, Rusty," Russ said. "Keep us in the cut."

"You don't know the way?" he asked, as he moved up to the bow.

"It probably hasn't changed since yesterday," Russ replied. "But it's a good idea if more than one knows the way."

Jesse could tell by the ripples on the water that there were numerous sandbars between where they were and the inlet, less than a quarter mile away.

The voice on the radio began the day's forecast. It would be warmer, close to seventy degrees, with decreasing winds out of the southeast, and seas running six to eight feet beyond the shoals.

"That's good, right?" Jesse asked. "Less wind?"

"It'll still be a rolly ride," Russ replied. "We're diving just inside the outer sandbar, which will dissipate the wave energy a lot, but make it choppier just inside the shoal. Whatever ship it is, I'm guessing it foundered on Outer Diamond Shoal during a storm, then sank in Diamond Slough, which separates Inner and Outer Diamond Shoals. Wind-driven waves travel all the way across the Atlantic, in deep water, so our little sandbar isn't much of an obstacle." He unlocked a small overhead compartment with a key, then took out a little black notebook. "Here, open this to the last page I wrote on, and enter the latitude and longitude into the Walker. It's pretty simple to figure out."

Jesse began thumbing through the pages as Russ undogged the front window and pushed it open a little.

He saw a few ships' names in the pages, along with some cryptic notes, and general or approximate locations. Some even had latitude and longitude numbers.

He found the last entry—*Suzanne*, August 1772, with lat and long numbers, and several notes that seemed to be written in code.

"The *Suzanne*?" he asked.

"That's her," Russ replied, turning into the current. "Not her real name, though. There's over five thousand wrecks out there, and only a small percentage have been found and even fewer identified."

Jesse bent close to the machine and entered the numbers Russ had written down for the boat he called *Suzanne*.

"Eighteen miles at a course of fifty-seven degrees," he said, reading the line below the numbers. "Roughly east-northeast. How long will that take?"

"A three-hour tour," Russ said in a sing-song voice, but off-key.

"A little to starboard," Rusty called back, but Russ was already turning the wheel.

"You and Walkley," Russ said, his voice lower. "And this is your former squad leader asking. What's going on between you?"

"Nothing really," Jesse said. "We went to a movie once, and out to dinner another time."

"The Corps doesn't have much restriction on enlisted Marines fraternizing," Russ said, "Just if there's a difference in rank. But you should be careful with her. She had a boyfriend back home, up until six months ago. He was killed in a car wreck."

"She never mention—"

"And maybe she won't," he interrupted. "But she told me and Suze one afternoon when we ran into her at the Brown-bagger having lunch. She's fragile right now, Jesse."

Jesse thought about it for a moment. The fact that Linda would tell Russ was improbable, but with Suzanne there....

"I won't mention it," he said. "And I'll be careful."

"Looks like ya need to come left a little," Rusty called out. "Then we'll be in the main channel."

"Thanks," Russ said, then pushed the throttle forward a little. "We're good from here on."

Rusty joined them in the enclosed pilothouse. "Colder'n a witch's heart out there," he said, rubbing his arms.

Russ reached up and changed the radio back to channel sixteen. "The forecast says it should warm to about seventy by noon. And out past the shoals, seas should be six to eight feet with a ten-second interval."

"Any idea how cold the water is?" Rusty asked.

Russ closed the front window. "I think it's around fifty-eight degrees."

Rusty visibly shivered. "When's it warm up?"

"To what you're used to?" Russ said. "Probably never. In August it'll get into the low eighties for a few weeks."

As they passed the two points of land, the incoming current became stronger, and the waves larger. Russ pushed the throttle forward and the boat picked up speed in relation to the water around them, crashing through the waves fairly easily and spraying foam out to both sides.

But they weren't going very fast at all, compared to the land.

After several minutes of pounding into wind, wave, and current, the current and wave interval diminished as Russ steered the boat from one marker to another.

"These cuts stay pretty consistent due to the tide flow in and out of the inlet," Russ said. "That is, unless a big hurricane moves through, but the shoals all around it are constantly changing. Mostly they're deep enough for *Dauntless*, though. She has a shallow draft and the tide's rising. So we ought to be good across the inner shoal waters."

"I wonder where that racing boat went last night," Jesse said. "We never did hear it again."

They'd sat out on the patio until past 2200, a good two hours after they'd heard the boat heading back, far in the distance.

"I bet they used up most of their gas comin' in," Rusty said. "So they gotta go easy headin' back to wherever they came from."

"With any luck," Russ said, "they got stopped by the Coasties and still had something on the boat."

Jesse turned and faced Russ. "You said you don't see that kind of boat around here?"

He laughed. "The OBX is mostly working people," he said. "Toys like that are too expensive. About the fastest boat you'll see around here is the ferry, and sport fishing boats. There's one operates here in Ocracoke and another in Hatteras, plus a few way up in Wanchese."

"So if the law or the Coast Guard saw one at a dock, they'd be suspicious."

"Suspicious and having enough probable cause to get a warrant are two different things," Russ said. "Any boat on the water can be stopped for a safety inspection. But unless they leave something out in plain sight, that's about it."

Rusty laughed. "Last year, a guy got busted durin' one of those safety checks. The dumbass had ten pounds of pot stashed under the sink in the head."

Russ also laughed. "And they checked that the holding tank's valve was closed, of course."

"Yep. The guy pretended he didn't know where the valve was and the FMP guy—that's the marine patrol down there—he said it was usually under the sink and opened it."

"I bet the three of us could write a book on all the dumb shit we've seen boaters do," Russ said, still chuckling.

"Me and a friend used to take a six-pack to the city marina," Rusty said. "We called it 'Dockside Follies.'"

"They almost caught one coming in Hatteras Inlet last summer," Russ said. "A Coast Guard high-speed utility boat was waiting just inside the inlet. They headed out to intercept when the drug boat was still a mile from the inlet, lights on and siren blaring. It was near dark, so the go-fast boat had to see it, and when it didn't slow, but started to veer away, the Coasties opened fire, and the guys on the drug boat tossed everything overboard as it sped away. Packages of cocaine washed up on the beach for days, all the way up to Virginia."

"They just throw it away?" Jesse asked. "We don't get a lot of this in Fort Myers."

"Any drugs comin' into Florida," Rusty began, "will come into the Keys. The quicker they can move it into a truck the better. And there's over a hundred miles of places to pull a truck over near a dock or beach."

Russ moved the throttle higher, and the engine chugged a little louder.

"We're clear of the sandbar," he said, as the bow plowed through another wave. It lifted the boat for a moment, then *Dauntless* surfed down the back side of the wave. "It'll be like this the rest of the way. The hardest part will be getting in and out of the water. I call it 'gorilla diving.'"

"Gorilla divin'?" Rusty asked.

"Once we're anchored in Diamond Slough," Russ began with a grin, "we'll have a good southerly current and be broadside to the waves. They won't be as big as outside the shoal, where the Gulf Stream is flowing a lot faster, but we'll have a two-knot current, and four-foot seas rolling in from the east. To move around and set up our gear, you'll want to be hunched over like an ape."

Rusty jerked a thumb toward Jesse. "Maybe *that* ape. We Thurmans have *evolved* on boats for the last five hundred years. We're built lower to the deck."

Chapter Thirteen

G etting out of the car, Ringo spotted the boat right away. There were only four in the marina; two were sailboats, one was a charter fishing boat, and the last was a big, fat, slow-looking trawler with a pilothouse raised above the main cabin.

Large, oval portholes all along the hull, except below the pilothouse, indicated it probably had cabins in front and back.

"Is that it?" he asked Roy, who'd driven them down from Hatteras to at least have a look.

Ringo figured if the boat wasn't what he was looking for, then there'd be no sense hanging around to talk to the owner. So, they partied at Roy's place, then crashed there for the night before making the short drive for a quick once-over.

"Yeah," Roy said, joining him at the front of the car. "All I know for sure is that it's fifty-three feet long."

"Can we go out on the dock?" Tim asked, as he and Moose joined them.

"I don't see why not," Roy replied, then led the way.

As they got closer, Roy pointed to a wooden plaque on the

side of the boat's cabin. "Okay, now we know two things. It's a fifty-three-foot Grand Alaskan, whatever that is."

"*Grand Alaskan* could be the name of the boat," Tim suggested, then corrected himself when the stern became visible. "Nope, it must be the builder. The name's *Nauti Gull*."

"Naughty girl," Moose said. "Dumb name."

The boat was huge. It wasn't much *longer* than Ringo's racing boat, but it was a lot wider and way taller, with a flybridge above the raised pilothouse, and probably the engine room below it.

As they walked out onto the dock the boat was tied up to, Ringo guessed the bimini top over the flybridge had to be at least fifteen feet above their heads.

"We're gonna need a bigger boat," Moose said.

Ringo ignored him. For the last four years, the big guy had been spouting that line from the movie *Jaws* every time he saw a boat. Not over and over, but every… single… time.

Tim moved farther along the dock toward the bow and could barely reach up to the deck. "You probably need some kinda special license to even drive one of these things."

"Not if you own it," a man said, sitting in a chair on the back of a boat tied opposite. "That boat belongs to Hal Gray."

He was wrinkled and his hair white, with a week's white stubble on his chin. He eyed them suspiciously.

"His brother, Pete, is a buddy of mine," Roy offered. "Pete told me Hal wanted to sell it, so we came to have a quick look. Hal's out—"

"Outta town, I know," the old man replied, getting to his feet. "He asked me to look after things. Name's Noble. Charlie Noble."

"What can you tell me about the boat, Mr. Noble?" Ringo asked. "I might be interested."

"DeFever design," the man replied, gripping one of the supports on his sailboat's bimini top. "It was built in '77 by American Marine, one of the last *wooden* boats they built."

"It's all wood?" Ringo asked.

"*Mostly* wood," he replied. "The hull and frames are oak, and the deck's teak," he replied. "The house is fiberglass, though."

"Any idea what's under the hood?" Tim asked.

"Twin John Deeres," he replied. "Naturally aspirated, 120 horses each."

"No speed demon then," Tim said. "This thing must weigh a ton."

The old man rolled his eyes as he stepped up onto his boat's side deck. "More like *thirty-six* tons, sonny. Speed ain't what a boat like that's built for. She carries near two *thousand* gallons of fuel and can cruise at six knots, nonstop, for more'n a week and over a thousand nautical miles."

Over a thousand miles, Ringo thought.

"Any idea what your friend's brother is asking for her?" Ringo asked Roy, who simply shrugged his shoulders.

"A hundred thousand dollars," the old man enunciated slowly. "Ya think ya can afford that?"

Ringo smiled at the old guy. Having just gotten paid for the run— in cash— he had more than that locked in Roy's car.

Of course, spending that would mean he might have to wait until the bank opened on Monday to pay Tim and Moose, but they'd understand.

The price was less than what he'd been planning to pay if he found the right boat, and if what the old man said was true, this one was already on the short list.

"That'll depend on how well it's equipped," Ringo said. "I plan to cruise long distances for extended periods."

The man looked him over for a moment. "Wait here," he said, then disappeared down into his sailboat.

When he came back up, he had a large blue thing in his hand with keys on it. "Hal left me the key, in case somethin' happened. Gimme enough cash for a case of beer and a bottle of rum and I'll show ya 'round the boat. I sorta helped him learn to run it."

"That'd be $18.65," Moose stated. They all turned toward him, and he pointed. "At the marina store over there. Not counting tax. I saw it on the sign."

Chapter Fourteen

———◆———◆———◆———◆———

"We should be right on top of it," Russ shouted from inside the wheelhouse.

Jesse was standing on the gunwale, hanging onto a grab rail as Rusty did the same on the other side of the boat. He scoured the water, trying to adjust his vision for twenty feet deeper than the water's surface.

It had gotten warmer, and with the engine below the wheelhouse, the inside had gotten uncomfortably hot until Russ opened the windows.

"Nothing yet," Jesse reported.

"Same here," Rusty replied.

"I'll start circling," Russ said, as the boat began turning in the big waves.

They were large, but spaced so far apart they were barely noticeable as the boat rose to meet them, heeling over slightly. But when the wave passed under the boat, it quickly rocked the other way, launching Jesse toward the wheelhouse or away from it.

Finally, after circling wider and wider for several minutes, Rusty shouted, "There! Thirty feet out at ten o'clock!"

The boat turned quickly, just as a wave passed under and the motion nearly tore Jesse's grip free.

"Watch the chain links!" Russ shouted. "They're marked every twenty feet and we're in ninety feet of water."

"Gotcha!" Rusty shouted, moving quickly to the bow.

Jesse stepped down and entered the pilothouse as Russ activated an electric windlass on the bow, lowering the giant anchor quickly.

"Forty feet!" Rusty called back, then a few seconds later, "Sixty!"

A few more seconds ticked by, then Rusty waved his hands. "End of the chain!"

Russ paused the windlass, allowing the slow drift of the boat to straighten out the last ten feet of chain resting on the seafloor with the anchor. Then he slowly let out the rope attached to the chain, allowing the boat drift with the current.

With a hundred feet of chain and four hundred feet of rope out, Rusty quickly attached a bridle to a loop near the end of the rode and headed back to the wheelhouse.

The boat slowly swung around until it was facing almost due north, into the current.

"I wouldn't back down on it too hard," Rusty advised through the open side curtain. "With the help of the current, it'd easily lift the chain and the hook."

"There's no need to back down at all," Russ said, shutting off the engine. "The first roller after all the chain was out straightened everything down there as the current carried us south. The rode didn't start pulling on the anchor until we had it all out. That anchor's buried a foot under the sand already; damned thing holds like you wouldn't believe."

"I doubt we drifted more than a few feet from where you left that float ball," Rusty said. "I could still see it when the chain hit eighty feet."

"It'll be due north of the anchor then," Russ said. "If the anchor I used on the float held."

Jesse wrote the current latitude and longitude down in Russ's notebook, just below the numbers he himself had written. The latitude was off by three seconds of arc, almost exactly the scope of the anchor rode. He'd check it again just before they got in the water.

"How's the float anchored?" Rusty asked.

Russ grinned. "It's tied to a cannon."

"Say what?"

"I think it's either an English warship," Russ began, "sunk in the early 1720s, or it might be from several years earlier— a Dutch ship that Blackbeard captured."

"No shit?" Rusty asked, his eyes wide.

"You guys okay with the roll?" Russ asked, nodding. "The wind and current's going to hold us beam to the sea the whole time we're here."

"Ya mean like sea *legs* or seasick?" Rusty asked. "'Cause I have one and never had the other."

"Yeah," Jesse said, "I don't get seasick either."

"Wanna eat lunch before we gear up, then?" Russ asked. "Best light on the bottom, what little there is, will be in less than an hour and won't last but two hours."

"A ninety-minute surface interval then," Jesse said. "Just sixty minutes will make the second dive a no-decomp dive."

"We'll do ten-minute safety stops just the same," Russ said. "On both dives. Eat now and wait for better viz?"

"Works for me," Rusty said. "Suzanne packs ya a good lunch?"

Russ knelt by the cooler, then looked up at Rusty. "I've seen you eat," he said, then tossed him a paper-wrapped bundle. "Does it matter?"

Rusty caught the package and started tearing it open. "Not particularly."

Russ handed one to Jesse. "BLTs, heavy on the B."

Jesse opened one end of the paper wrapping and bit into the thick sandwich, made with some kind of roll—wheat, he guessed. The rest of his sandwich stood little chance.

All three finished in just a few minutes, then slowly began to set up their gear in the pitching seas. Russ had been right; staying low to the deck was key when the rollers passed under the boat. Huge waves were breaking over the sandbar half a mile away, expending most of their energy on the shoal before growing again as they crossed the deeper water between the sandbars— what Russ had called Diamond Slough.

Russ pulled up the bridle and clipped a long line to it with a float ball attached to the other end—a tag line to make it easier to get to the anchor line against the current.

"Let's get wet," he said, then sat in front of his gear, slipped his arms through the shoulder straps, and cinched the chest and waist straps. "Roll backward on this side and use the tag line. You'll wear yourself out trying to swim against this current."

Jesse sat down on the bench next to him and put his fins on first, then pulled his mask down over his face to dangle below his chin before strapping himself into his BC.

Russ waited until a wave passed under the boat, then stood and used the grab rail to help him step up backward onto the bench and sit on the gunwale. Then he rolled backward off the boat.

Jesse slid over to his spot, put his mask on, and stuck the regulator's second stage in his mouth, breathing around it to conserve the air in the tank.

With one hand on the rail, he stood and waited for the next wave before stepping up backward onto the seat as Russ had done. He added some air to his BC with the auto-inflator, then waited for the next wave to pass.

When he rolled back off the boat and into the water, the cold hit him instantly, causing a moment of shock, which he'd anticipated. He quickly shook it off and power-kicked toward the side of the boat and the tag line.

Although they'd trained outdoors in sub-zero conditions for days on end, it was totally different in cold water—it sapped away body heat a lot faster than air, and a person could get hypothermic in even eighty-degree water. In just sixty-degree water, a person without protection would have little chance of surviving more than a few hours. The cold would numb the body, then the brain would become foggy, and the victim would simply fall asleep, slip below the surface, and drown.

Chapter Fifteen

————◆———◆———◆———◆————

Back home in Fort Myers, water sports and outdoor activities didn't end in winter. Jesse had done a lot of winter diving, usually with a thin wetsuit, but never in water below sixty-five degrees. He knew from experience that if he were even to be able to function at all, he'd need to stay warmer than the water around him.

Moving quickly, Jesse pulled himself forward on the tag line to give Rusty room to roll backward from the same spot. He paused and took a deep breath before pulling the collar of his new wetsuit away from his neck, allowing his wetsuit to flood with cold water.

The shock hit him again.

He knew that getting water *inside* the wetsuit, where his body heat would quickly warm it, was key to being at least moderately comfortable for the rest of the dive.

Hearing a loud splash, Jesse looked back and saw Rusty righting himself. Then he looked forward and saw Russ, kicking his fins and pulling on the tag line.

So, he started doing the same thing after he glanced back again to spot Rusty on the tag line right behind him. When they reached the front of the boat, where the line connected to the bridle, they paused for a second, exchanging okay signs before they started their descent.

In unison, they raised their purge valves over their heads and released the air from their BCs. Jesse felt his weight belt pulling him down as he held onto the anchor line just above Russ.

The water had a lot of suspended sediment, so the anchor line was only visible for about fifteen or twenty feet below them.

Russ descended first and Jesse followed, hitting the auto-inflator now and then, releasing short bursts of pressurized air from his tank into the BC to compensate for the increased water pressure which squeezed the volume of air in the BC's bladder smaller as they descended. He did the same with his inner ears, by holding his nose with his free hand every four or five feet and exhaling against it, equalizing his inner ear pressure.

It would've been preferable for each of them to descend on three sides of the anchor line so they could see each other, but that would have been impossible in the current. So they were stacked one above the other, all facing into the current like flapping pennants on a mast.

As they went down and forward following the anchor line, the sediment decreased, but so did the available light from the sun, so Jesse thought maybe the sediment was still there but not visible.

It was an easy descent, kicking slightly to keep a hand on the anchor line as they went down, and moving forward steadily as they descended.

Russ progressed down very slowly, a long, slow stream of air coming from his second stage about every fifteen seconds as he controlled his breathing and body movement to use as little air as possible. He kicked slowly, pulling himself deeper with his hands.

He only had two metal detectors, so it had been agreed that since Jesse had never used one, Rusty would carry the second one, and Jesse would carry the "goodie" bag with the hand shovels and a small prybar, plus the float and the anchor it was attached to, once they found it.

Besides those tools, each of them had a long knife strapped to the inside of one leg and a shorter blade attached upside down to their BC shoulder straps. Each also had a small dive light secured to the other shoulder strap, though it was unlikely they'd need them.

Once they reached the bottom, visibility was less than ten feet, and when Jesse saw the anchor line lifting and dropping a couple of feet of chain to the sandy bottom, he realized that finding the float's anchor might not be as easy as he thought it'd be.

The current on the bottom was considerably less, and they easily swam against it, just above the anchor chain, Russ in the lead and Jesse and Rusty swimming side by side behind and slightly above him.

Jesse looked around as he swam. There was nothing but sand. In every direction, just sand. No rocks, no corals, no sea fans, and no fish. It was like they were flying slowly over a desert.

After about thirty feet, the chain disappeared, covered by sand.

Russ paused and turned toward Jesse and Rusty, giving an

okay sign, which they returned. Then he looked back at the visible chain and checked the compass on his wrist.

Turning around, he struck out on a reciprocal heading, finning at a faster-than-moderate pace, and Jesse knew instantly why. He was measuring distance by time at a consistent two knots, speed over ground, turning the power up to counter the slight current.

It was a trick he'd taught them in underwater nav class, instructing them to recognize a specific speed over ground, and train harder so they could swim at that SOG, regardless of current speed.

So, they'd spent countless hours in the long, narrow training pool, with its massive water pumps, wearing full dive and combat gear, finning against a man-made current until each man in the squad could maintain their position in a five-knot current for fifteen minutes—equal to a mile-and-a-quarter-swim in calm water. Just getting to that speed with all their gear was no easy feat, and they'd learned to better streamline their bodies and equipment in the process.

Maintaining that speed had been grueling. But they all knew that, if need be, they could move forward at a steady two knots against a strong three-knot current.

Russ was swimming against the current at two knots, speed over ground, to measure the remaining distance to the boat's anchor. Jesse'd already seen the markings on the anchor chain for eighty feet about halfway between the end and where the chain disappeared under the sand, so if he was right, they'd find the anchor sixty feet ahead, or in less than half a minute.

Jesse spotted a mound of sand just ahead of Russ, and beyond it, a straight trench. He recognized it as the area where their anchor had dragged for a few feet before burying itself in the sandy bottom, creating the bulge.

Russ angled toward the mound, then continued straight, following the drag mark and giving them the signal to fan out.

Jesse angled away to the right, sweeping his head and eyes back and forth, and keeping Russ within sight. With Rusty out of sight on the other side, they'd increased the width of their visibility from ten feet on either side, to twenty.

Suddenly, Jesse spotted the line. It had a white streamer tied ten feet off the bottom. He might not have seen it otherwise, since the line was so thin.

He reached back and rapped his knuckles on his tank, then when Russ looked, he pointed. Russ motioned to Rusty, then Jesse started swimming slowly toward the float's anchor tether, giving Russ and Rusty time to catch up without losing sight of him.

Jesse hovered near the bottom, lightly finning into the current, where what he could now see was paracord disappearing into the sand.

But Russ had said that he'd tied it to a cannon.

Russ swam up alongside Jesse, then pulled lightly on the line, lifting a large lead weight out of the sand.

Another length of paracord was attached to the sinker. He gave it a slight tug and it came loose from the weight. Then he handed the lead anchor to Jesse and started swimming, gently pulling the other line up out of the sand as he went.

Two minutes later, a long object could be seen sticking up out of the bottom with the end of the paracord tied to it in the same way the sinker had been—one slight tug would untie it.

Russ had set up a simple diversion in case someone saw the float and dove down to have a look.

Chapter Sixteen

◆━━━◆━━━◆━━━◆

R uss had already given them the basic plan for the dive. He'd also told them that he'd ended his last search on the east side of the cannon and had already covered a good bit to the south, the side they'd approached from.

He'd said that if it hadn't been disturbed, he'd expect to find more to the west of the cannon, due to the direction it was pointed—west being inboard on the sunken ship.

But he'd also warned them that assuming the cannon hadn't moved in the last three hundred hurricane seasons would be ridiculous. So he'd assigned Rusty the area immediately south, and he took the west side.

Jesse checked his watch and noted they'd already used three minutes of the fifteen Russ had said they could spend. Having little else to do, Jesse got one of the hand shovels out and began waving it at the sand in random places, kicking it up in clouds that settled down-current.

It wasn't long before he started hearing a subdued beeping

and looked around. Russ was also looking, but Rusty was waving his detector back and forth over a spot.

Jesse swam over to him and offered him the hand shovel, then dug a second one out and together, they started digging in the loose sand, most of which cascaded back in the hole. So they widened the area to dig, and Rusty passed the detector over the spot again.

They started digging some more, and after several minutes, Jesse's shovel hit something hard, and they both heard it.

Digging furiously, they soon uncovered a large, very ancient-looking rock that was encrusted with dead barnacles.

Russ swam over, pointed at the cannon, then made a gun-firing motion with his thumb and index finger while pointing at the rock.

A cannonball.

A three-hundred-year-old cannonball.

Rusty shrugged his shoulders and went back to detecting as Russ returned to where he'd been working.

Most cannonballs were just solid iron, and when fired, simply mowed down everything in their path, be it a ship's hull, frames, masts, rigging, or crew.

In medieval times, huge battles were fought with troops lined up across a valley, row upon row deep, and a good cannoneer could make the ball skip over the ground, taking out dozens of troops.

There was little chance that the ancient ball was explosive, and zero chance of it being able to detonate if it was, so Jesse ignored it and started using two trowels to fan away the sand.

It did have some historical value, he thought, as he stirred up the silty bottom. Knowing what size guns the boats had could identify the wreck. So he planned to bring it to the surface after the second dive.

After several minutes of fanning, something tumbled and disappeared as sand fell over it. Jesse sifted through the soft sand and found it, pulling out a bright, shiny gold coin, just like Russ had in his shop.

An English guinea!

He tapped the two small shovels together to get Russ and Rusty's attention, then held the coin up.

Russ came over to him and took the goodie bag, a canvas bag with a mesh bottom for water to drain from, and a large half-round stiff wire opening at the top that could clasp closed to hold fish and lobster in.

He opened it and showed Jesse a zippered canvas pouch that had been sewn to the inside. He unzipped it, and held it open for Jesse, who dropped the coin in.

Russ gave him a thumbs-up, pumping his hand vigorously. Then they went back to work, Russ and Rusty using the metal detectors to methodically search the area around the cannon.

Jesse continued fanning the sand, amazed that it'd been so easy to find. One coin in the whole Atlantic Ocean, and he'd found it.

Russ's machine started pinging, and Jesse went over to him with the hand shovels ready.

After a few minutes of digging, they found a clump of what looked like oyster shells, nearly a foot long and six or eight thick. Russ pointed at the goodie bag and Jesse opened it so he could drop the clump in. It looked a lot like the one in Russ's shop that he thought was a cache of silver coins.

Not as valuable as gold, but still treasure.

Gold was so dense, nothing could grow on it, or attach to it, so even after three hundred years buried in the sand on the sea floor, the guinea looked just as bright and shiny as the day it was struck.

Jesse thought for a moment about the man who'd once owned the coin. Was he a British sailor? An officer maybe? It was unlikely a common sailor would have something so valuable. Or was it pirate treasure, stolen from a British merchantman?

Jesse kept an eye on his dive watch, a cheap one he'd picked up at a dive shop in the Keys. They'd been at the bottom for thirteen minutes and it was almost time to surface. He still had a good thousand pounds of air, so that wasn't a concern.

Rusty's detector went off again, and this time, Russ didn't wait but swam straight over, knowing their time at the bottom was almost over.

All three of them began to dig. After a moment, another gold coin tumbled from Rusty's shovel.

He picked it up and excitedly motioned for the goodie bag as Russ passed his detector over the spot again.

It beeped.

They dug some more and unearthed two more coins. Further probes didn't set off the detector, so Russ pointed a finger upward, calling an end to their first dive.

They'd found four guineas and what might be a bunch of silver coins.

The ascent was simple. They allowed the current to carry them back to the anchor line as they slowly rose, then they just followed the line up until they reached fifteen feet. Russ stopped them there and checked his dive watch. He held up three fingers, then folded them over his thumb, signaling three

minutes. Then he showed both of them his air pressure gauge—
over a thousand pounds. Jesse and Rusty showed their gauges, as
well. Jesse was only slightly under that, and Rusty still had nearly
twelve hundred psi showing on his.

All three men knew the standard Navy dive tables backward
and forward, and fifteen minutes was less than the no-decom-
pression limit at the depth they'd gone. The short stop was just
for safety purposes, to let a little nitrogen off-gas from the bloodstream before surfacing.

The most dangerous part of a dive, as far as nitrogen
bubbles forming in the bloodstream, was from fifteen feet to the
surface.

Every thirty feet of depth was equal to another atmosphere
of pressure, so at thirty feet, the pressure was two atmospheres,
double what it was at the surface, and at sixty feet it was triple.

But the greatest percentage increase based on depth was the
top fifteen feet, with a fifty percent increase in pressure. The next
fifteen feet took a diver from 1.5 to 2 atmospheres of pressure,
an increase of only thirty-three percent.

Finally, Russ, who was at the bottom of the stack, motioned
for them to surface.

"Hot damn!" Rusty shouted as soon as his head bobbed to
the surface beside Jesse. "We found gold, man!"

"If that clump is silver coins, like I figure," Russ said, letting
the current carry him along the side of the boat, "then there's
likely a good ten or twenty in there."

"What are silver coins worth?" Jesse asked.

"Depends on what kind they are," Russ replied, pulling his
fins off and tossing them aboard. "The Brits used silver for
shillings and pennies, and they were minted every few years by

each successive English sovereign. Some kings and queens didn't reign long, so fewer coins were struck with their likeness. King Philip ruled England for just four years, while Elizabeth I ruled for more than forty."

He climbed up the folding ladder with his BC and tank on, as Jesse and Rusty removed their fins and handed them up.

"Ballpark?" Rusty asked as he climbed aboard.

Russ grabbed his hand and helped him over the transom. "Anywhere from ten bucks to maybe a hundred, depending on condition."

Jesse climbed up and accepted Rusty's hand, then stepped over into the boat, careful to time it between waves.

"I knew this was going to be a hot spot," Russ said, sitting on the bench and shrugging out of his BC. "Let's have a look at those guineas."

Chapter Seventeen

———◆——◆——◆——◆———

A s the three of them sat on the deck in the cockpit with the gear, Jesse couldn't help thinking how lucky they'd been. They'd found the final resting place of a three-hundred-year-old wreck in a matter of minutes, and dug at least $3,000 worth of coins from the sand where she rested.

Well, *Russ* had *found* it; he and Rusty were just along for the ride.

Jesse unclipped the goodie bag from his BC and pulled it closer to where he sat. One by one, he took the coins out and handed them to Russ, who gave each a quick examination.

"All struck in 1680," he said. "The dates of the silver coins might determine which ship is down there, though."

Rusty looked over. "How so?"

"Whichever ship it is," Russ replied with a grin, "it had to have sunk *after* 1680. Shillings and pennies were way more common and what the average person carried and used to buy things with, so crewmen on a warship were unlikely to have gold."

"I get it," Rusty said. "A common sailor would likely have pennies in his pocket, and they were likely newer."

"Exactly," Russ said. "Finding silver goes a lot farther in establishing the date of the wreck."

Rusty chuckled as he picked up one of the guineas. "Yeah, but they don't look near as pretty."

"Keep it if you want," Russ said. "We found four, and each of you gets a fourth."

"Hell *yeah*," Rusty said. "I know a jeweler in Key Weird who specializes in mounting doubloons and such."

"Who would have *gold* coins on a warship?" Jesse asked.

"The captain and officers might have a few," Russ replied, digging through the cooler. "The ship's purser would be responsible for any large cache of gold coins onboard, to buy provisions with."

He pulled out a Tupperware container and opened it. "Pineapple," he said, taking a couple of chunks and passing the bowl. "Gets the salty taste out."

"How much do ya think might be down there?" Rusty asked, taking a whole slice. "Thanks."

Russ wiped his mouth with the back of his hand and grinned. "The purser would have a whole chest of gold coins, probably as big as this cooler."

Rusty gaped at him. "That'd be hundreds of pounds! To buy provisions with?"

Russ nodded. "Feeding a couple hundred men for a month at sea wasn't cheap."

"Nobody else knows about this?" Jesse asked, looking all around and feeling a little apprehensive.

"Not even Suze knows the location," Russ replied. "The only

place I've written it is in my notebook, and it's kept locked up when here on the boat, or at home in my office."

"It's a pretty flat bottom here," Jesse said. "Any kind of profile, even a cannon sticking out of the sand, is bound to draw fish."

Russ nodded. "Someone might've stumbled on that cannon using a depth finder. You saw the bottom topography. And there's likely more. If the ship broke up on the shoal, parts of it would've rained down here in the slough, covering a huge area."

"And if the wreck is one of Teach's ships?" Rusty asked.

"At the peak of his pirating career," Russ began, "Black-beard had five ships, mostly smaller one-and two-masted sloops. And he didn't send them all out marauding at once. At least not often. One report says that one of his sloops sailed up to Virginia for supplies and never returned. So it could be that one."

"What would be the best way to nail down which ship it is?" Jesse asked. "Do they know all the ships that sank around here?"

"Not even a tenth," Russ replied, taking another pineapple chunk from the bowl and popping it in his mouth. "Finding a brass ship's bell with the name engraved on it would be the best identification. As far as where a ship sank, *if* they had time to deploy a longboat and *if* there were survivors, and *if* they could sail to shore, the name of the ship would've been known, as well as the general area she went down. But exactly *where* it sank?" He shook his head. "Only a handful of officers ever knew their position, and a longboat in a storm could drift for miles in the Gulf Stream."

"What if they didn't have time to launch a boat?" Jesse asked.

"We're eight or so miles from Cape Hatteras," Russ replied, with a serious expression. "Catastrophes happen suddenly. Without a boat, survivors were unlikely, since most sailors at the time couldn't swim, and even if they could... it's *eight* miles. This wreck could just as easily be one of the thousands transiting the area that just never arrived at their destination. Every ship passing Cape Hatteras comes close to these shoals. Northbound vessels ride the Stream, passing just a mile or so outside the outer shoal. A lot of them come too close. Any ship going south would either be way offshore, beyond the Gulf Stream, or they'd run in close and try to make it through Diamond Slough here."

Jesse nodded. "The Gulf Stream can be pretty rough, I hear. I've only encountered it down in the Keys with Rusty."

"Imagine heading south and rounding the Cape in even a moderate southeasterly gale," Russ said. "That means sailing across the Stream, then tacking back toward shore once you were clear of the Cape and shoals."

"And the whole while," Rusty said, shuddering, "the Stream's carryin' 'em north. One miscalculation and they might turn and run right up on the shoal here, thinking they were farther to the south."

"A smaller coastal vessel heading north and staying inside the Gulf Stream wouldn't have it easy either," Jesse said. "They'd be forced to jibe and sail east into the Gulf Stream and that'd put the current, wind, and waves all right on their beam, each trying to drive the ship onto the shoal."

The boat rolled to one side as a large wave passed under it, and the bow slapped down on the water, punctuating Jesse's words.

"Let's get our gear switched over," Russ said. "I want to get back down there."

"It hasn't been an hour," Jesse advised. "Not that it matters much."

"Which is why I dive a conservative profile," Russ said. "Second dive, we'll do the same bottom time and safety stop. Agreed?"

Jesse looked at his watch and nodded. "It'll actually *be* a deco stop this time, with just thirty minutes of surface interval."

The longer the surface interval was between dives, the more nitrogen was off-gassed from the blood through regular breathing. But there would still be some residual nitrogen buildup when a diver went down on a second dive, unless they spent several hours at the surface. That excess buildup was factored into the dive tables and could either shorten the amount of time at depth on a subsequent dive, or require a mandatory decompression stop at fifteen feet. Or both.

Rusty was looking at his plastic repetitive dive table, running a finger down a column on the back. "Yep, just like he said. We gotta cut it to thirteen minutes at the bottom or do a five-minute deco stop at fifteen feet."

Russ laughed. "Hey, what's that cyborg's name on *Get Smart*? You know... the robot guy."

"Hymie!" Rusty exclaimed. "He was bullet-proof and knew everything. Yeah, Jesse even favors him some."

Russ laughed again. "Get your gear switched over. We'll do fifteen on the bottom again, with the decompression stop. I'll go move the tag line to the other side of the boat."

Just as he started to rise, a wave passed under the boat, lifting it above the surrounding ocean, and out of the corner of his eye, Jesse caught a quick glimpse of something red behind them.

Russ stepped up onto the gunwale, and before Jesse could shout a warning, there was a sudden roar and a crash of water as a bright red boat flew past no more than ten feet away, turning hard to avoid colliding.

Jesse reached for Russ's hand as he and Rusty both sprang to their feet. He missed by inches, as the wake from the speeding boat hit *Dauntless* and nearly swamped them, sending Russ tumbling into the water.

"Son of a bitch!" he shouted, gasping for air as the current started carrying him away.

Russ easily grabbed the tag line behind the boat and began pulling himself hand-over-hand to get back to the stern.

"You okay?" Rusty shouted, reaching down to help him up the ladder and back on deck.

Keeping a good grip on the grab rail, Jesse climbed onto the gunwale and looked out past the bow. The racing boat's twin-engines screamed as it roared away to the south. He caught a glimpse of it several times between rollers, flying off the wave tops like it was out of control.

Russ moved over beside him. "Was that the same—"

"No," Jesse replied, watching as the boat disappeared over the horizon. "The one we saw last night was dark blue. That one was red."

Chapter Eighteen

————◆—◆——◆—◆————

Aside from the name, *Nauti Gull* was exactly what Ringo was looking for, perhaps even more so, and the price was less than he'd figured on paying. It was two years old, the engines only had 210 hours on them, which equated to about two hours of run time per week—a dock queen meant to impress the hometown crowd.

On top of that, the owner had become sick and was struggling to make the payments. To Ringo, it sounded desperate and his natural shark-like business instincts kicked in.

The old sailor, Charlie Noble, had told him "in confidence" that Hal Gray was barely going to be able to pay off what he owed even if he got what he was asking, so Ringo shouldn't expect a lot of wiggle room.

They ended the two-hour tour of the boat way down in the engine room, which was below the pilothouse. Charlie had been very thorough, and seemed to know all the boat's systems and maintenance requirements, which Tim absorbed like a sponge.

"Besides the way we came in from the hallway to the

forward cabin," Charlie said, as he walked between the engines to the back of the engine room, "you can also get in through this hatch from the lazarette, that big storage area under the cockpit deck I showed ya earlier."

"I've heard some good things about these engines," Tim said.

Charlie put a hand on top of each engine. "These are 'bout the simplest motors you can find. They're bullet-proof, as long as you change the oil and filters regular."

Ringo had heard in boating circles just how reliable the John Deere marine engines were. Charlie went on to explain that they had no electronic gizmos, no turbochargers, a simple fuel delivery system, and the lines from the fuel tanks ran through a polishing system to ensure it was as free of contaminants as possible.

"That's a serious thing in many third-world areas," Charlie told them. "In a lot of places, diesel's sold on the black market just as much as at a pump. I always strain fuel through a filter when I pour it into my tank in places like that."

"What if you were to just run one motor?" Tim asked. "Like, if you were makin' a really long trip."

Charlie rubbed the stubble on his chin. "We tested her at six knots cruisin' speed over a long trip and she averaged 1.1 nautical miles per gallon. If ya run the tanks bone dry, that's twenty-two hundred miles, minus whatever ya might burn runnin' the generator."

"Two thousand?" Ringo asked.

"I'd keep five hundred gallons in reserve and never plan a trip longer than fifteen hundred. But if ya was to go slower, ya might get a tad better, and if ya alternate engines, and ya really don't wanna just run one all the time, to keep the hours the same... I'd bet she could go a good bit farther... maybe two thousand miles. Course, ya could always just carry a couple dozen jerry cans in that lazarette."

"Do you have any way of contacting Mr. Gray?" Ringo asked. "I'd like to have a sea trial."

"I got a number," Charlie said. "If one of you guys come with me to the marina store and carry my beer and rum back, I'll give him a call."

"Go with him, Moose," Ringo said, as they went back into the hall, then up the steps to the pilothouse. "Do you mind if Tim and I wait here?"

"Suit yourself," Charlie said. "We're hooked up to shore power, so feel free to turn anything on to check that it works."

"Think this is it?" Tim asked, after Charlie and Moose left. "It's a nice boat and all, but slower than a slug, man."

"Did you ever see a slug, then a few minutes later, look at where he was and not find him?" Ringo turned on the gauges for the helm. The fuel tanks were nearly full. "I can turn these keys, disappear, and not be seen again until a week later way down in Nassau, all the way out to Bermuda, or north to Canada."

Tim nodded. "Yeah, man. With one very thirsty boat when ya get there. You know what 2,000 gallons of diesel will run? You're talkin' a grand every time you fill up."

"With what I've piled up," Ringo said, "I can run those engines down there all day for the rest of my life and never worry about it."

"And go where?" Tim asked, switching on the radar. "With a

range of fifteen-hundred miles, you're not crossing any oceans or anything."

"Don't bet on it," Ringo said. "A boat like this could make it from Greenland to Sweden in the summer. That's only about eight or nine hundred miles, and would open up four whole continents."

"Four?" Tim said. "Europe, Africa, Asia… What else? If you're plannin' to go to Antarctica, count me out on that leg."

"Australia's also a continent," Ringo replied. "Getting across to Sweden would open up all of Europe, Africa, Asia, and Australia for me." He grinned. "But why not Antarctica?"

"Check this out," Tim said, adjusting the radar for maximum range.

On the screen, well offshore, the radar reflection from two boats could be seen. Ringo looked in that direction. The pilothouse sat so high, he could look across the narrow island and see the whitecaps out on the ocean.

"They're twelve miles away," Tim said. "You can't see 'em."

"Is that—"

"Carlos and Trina," Tim said. "No other boats out there could be going that fast."

"How can you tell how fast they're going?"

"Experience, man," Tim said. "Remember, I was a radar tech in the Air Force. I can guess from each subsequent return that those two boats out there are making at least sixty miles an hour."

"I don't know which is worse," Ringo said, still gazing out toward the ocean. "My old life as a slave to corporate America, or the current one being a slave to a Colombian cartel."

Tim nodded and followed his gaze. "At least a corporate exec won't slit your throat and pull your tongue out."

Ringo grinned. "Don't bet on that, either."

He was right, though. The corporate world was cutthroat, but usually only figuratively. If you came out on the bad end of a deal, you only lost your house and savings, not your life.

Ringo had once borne the trappings of an upscale professional—the cars, the houses, the boats. What he didn't have was the excitement he'd felt as a younger executive, thirsty for the opportunity to reach the top.

Then he'd found boat racing through a corporate takeover, and rather than dismantle the business, he'd put money into it, buying out other similar businesses as he gained popularity as a racing boat driver. It was through contacts there that he was approached about making a dope run, which at the time had seemed very exciting.

Now, at forty-one, he was a seasoned, in-demand smuggler, earning enough on every run to pay his crew, his overhead, and all his bills. And every month, he was still setting aside at least as much as he'd made in a year behind the desk.

"Put it over on my boat," Charlie's voice called from outside.

Ringo went to the door as the old man climbed back aboard and saw Moose loading the guy's boat with the booze.

"I talked to Hal," Charlie said. "He's actually cuttin' his trip short and will be home later this afternoon. Can ya be ready by three?"

Ringo looked over at Roy. "Do you have to get back to Hatteras?"

"Anything I got goin' on will keep," he replied. "In the meantime, we can go over to the pub and get something to eat."

"And maybe a coupla beers?" Charlie asked.

Chapter Nineteen

———◆———◆———◆———◆———

After a few minutes and several calls on the radio from Russ, it was obvious that the boat wasn't coming back to see if anyone was injured in the near miss.

Jesse knew the driver had seen them, otherwise he wouldn't have taken evasive action and likely would have at least sideswiped *Dauntless*.

"Pretty rough conditions for a joyride," Rusty said, after Russ hung up the mic.

"Another drug runner," Russ grumbled angrily.

"What are the chances of seeing two of them in less than twenty-four hours?" Jesse asked.

"I've been thinking on that," Russ replied. "Remember how I said everyone thinks they come from a cargo ship? They get checked over pretty good coming into port. But what if they had a fleet of fast boats available that could pick up smaller quantities at sea to bring to shore?"

Rusty shook his head. "A fleet? Those things are expensive, man; just one is close to six figures."

"But what if the boats were all owned by different people?" Russ asked. "Private shuttlers. You called them cocaine cowboys, but to afford one of those, you'd need a top-level executive's income."

"A bunch of bored businessmen?" Jesse asked.

"Why not?" Rusty agreed. "Once the thrill of the deal wears off, they look for somethin' else."

"But turning to drug smuggling?"

"Once a person crosses that line, they lose the protection of just being an innocent bystander," Russ said. "That shit destroys lives. Again, if we had a thumper, that boat *and* the lowlife crew would be at the bottom right now."

"You'd actually do that?" Jesse asked without thinking.

Marines were notorious for tough talk, but he knew Russ could back it up with extreme action. For the last four months, he'd been their mentor, teaching his squad, especially the two new guys, everything he knew about small unit tactics, both from the book and from the jungle.

Russ looked at him for a moment. "I don't honestly know," he finally replied with a sigh. "I know I'd like to. People who are involved in that shit probably chose a path of crime years ago, and more often than not, they'll die by the sword. Any day's as good as another to die. Nobody'd miss them."

Jesse knew all too well what Russ meant. Three months earlier, he'd ended the life of a man who likely would have gone down in a gunfight with police, possibly taking someone else with him.

Jesse had struggled with it at first. But that didn't last long once he'd learned all there was to know about Sideshift Briscoe. He'd terrorized, bullied, and raped more than a dozen women that were known, getting many of them hooked on drugs and then prostituting them out.

His time in prison hadn't rehabilitated him. It was just a matter of time before he would have died by someone else's hand. By being the instrument of his demise, Jesse had probably saved future victims.

As Russ turned toward his gear, Jesse looked over at Rusty, knowing his friend was thinking the same thing. They'd both promised, along with Juliet and Gina, never to mention it to anyone. The cops had taken responsibility and that was that.

"I killed a man on New Year's Day," Jesse said without thinking, but knowing he could trust his squad leader.

Russ stopped unscrewing the first stage of his regulator from the tank and slowly turned to face Jesse. "You did what?"

"It's a long story," Rusty said softly. "I was with him. We were workin' with the cops."

Russ turned and sat down beside the cooler, one arm draped over it as he looked back and forth at them. Then he opened the cooler, took out three beers, and passed them around. "We're done diving for the day. I want to hear all about this."

So, they sat down on the deck and Jesse and Rusty began recounting the run-in they'd had with Briscoe and his gang, then had to back up to the altercation with Briscoe's cousin, Bear Bering, which had landed the gang leader in prison for murder, allowing Sideshift to take control of the biker gang.

Only Briscoe was never really in *full* control.

They first told him about the several attempts made on a Navy man's life, and the porn star who'd been behind the attempted murders, trying to lure the Navy guy's wife into the porn business.

They ended the story with the deaths of Brisco and the woman who'd been manipulating the gang leader, Amber Henderson.

"And she was behind it all?" Russ asked. "The porn star?"

"Turns out, she controlled the whole gang," Rusty said. "The cops shot her, but Jesse's kick definitely killed the biker dude."

"And the cops took full responsibility?" Russ asked. "I've heard stories that the Key West police aren't the straightest."

"The Florida Keys ain't Key Weird," Rusty said. "This was the Monroe County Sheriff's Office and Bart Johnson's solid. He convinced the other cops to accept his version of what happened, that he himself had shot Sideshift in the head and killed him."

"But wouldn't an autopsy—"

"The coroner who did it is related to Bart," Rusty said, shaking his head. "Briscoe's *official* cause of death was a gunshot to the head from Bart's service weapon. He was suspended with pay for a few days, and went fishin' on the county's dime, but the shootin' was ruled justified, and he's back on duty."

Russ took a slow pull from his beer can, then looked across the cockpit at each of them. "That's exactly what I meant. That Briscoe guy was imprisoned for rape? And as soon as he got out, he started in with porn and prostitution?" He shook his head. "His course was set a long time before you met him, Jesse. In my book, he got off easy. How does what happened affect you emotionally?"

Rusty and Jesse looked at one another.

"Emotionally?" Jesse asked.

Russ shrugged. "It's something I've been working on with

Suze; getting in touch with my emotions. What I mean is, are you okay with knowing that you killed a man?"

"It's what we train to do," Jesse replied.

"We're trained to kill the *enemy*," Russ said. "With a heart as cold as Arctic ice. But we're not law enforcement."

Jesse shrugged. "Vigilante justice?" Then he looked Russ squarely in the eye. "I stepped on a roach."

Russ nodded. "Exactly how I feel about these drug runners."

"Knowin' that," Rusty said, arching an eyebrow, "we'd like ya to keep this to yourself."

"If you can't," Jesse added, "I'll understand and respect your decision. I just felt like you should know."

Russ studied Jesse for a moment, as if trying to see something in him that wasn't visible.

"You were helping the police," Russ said. "Rusty tells me the deputy's a stand-up guy and I believe it. Who am I to second-guess his decision? I wasn't there." He glanced at Rusty for a moment, then back to Jesse. "*Had* I been there, I'd like to think I would have stood right beside you."

Chapter Twenty

————◆——◆——◆——◆——

Suzanne and Russel Junior were waiting on the dock when *Dauntless* came through the inlet and turned into the cut that led back to the dock. Russ had called her on the radio when they were close enough.

"Did you find anything?" she asked, as Russ reversed the engine, and Jesse and Rusty stepped off with dock lines.

"Another possible cluster of silver coins," Russ replied after he shut off the engine. Then he stepped up onto the dock beside her. "And four more guineas."

"You're back early," she said, reaching up on her toes to kiss him.

"A drug boat almost slammed into us," Russ said. "So we decided to abort the second dive. We found all that on the first one, and it was Jesse and Rusty who found the guineas."

"I looked in the tub with the first clump," she said. "I'm pretty sure it's a bunch of coins and some other things."

"Let's go have a look," Russ suggested, then squatted down to the toddler's level. "Who's the best treasure hunter around?"

"You, Dada!" the boy replied enthusiastically.

"Oh, Jesse," Suzanne said, "Your grandfather called, and we talked for a few minutes. He sounds so sweet. Anyway, I gave him the location of the house and he's going to have his friend fly over real low to let us know they're here."

"He can do that so close to the airstrip?" Jesse asked.

Russ laughed as he opened the door to the shop. "There *might* be a plane a week land here this time of year. Sometimes three or four in the summer."

They went inside and headed straight to the tub that held the big clump. Russ placed the goodie bag on the table next to it, and before doing anything else, started mixing water and salt in another clean tub.

"Pull that clump out, Jesse," he said, as he began to stir. "And set it right in here. Exposure to air too soon isn't good."

"What about the guineas?" Rusty asked.

"Put them in here too," Russ replied, as Jesse lowered the encrusted mass into the tub. "If you want, you can take one of those from yesterday."

"Naw," he said, "I'll wait for the one I found."

Russ looked up at him as the water flowed into the tub. "How do you know which one it is?"

Rusty moved his finger along the side of his nose. "Chuck's got a cut on that big ol' beak of his."

"Chuck?" Jesse asked. "Oh… King Charles."

"Shut the water off once it's over the cluster," Russ told Jesse, then moved to the tub with the cluster from the previous day. "That saltwater flush is less than half the salinity of the ocean. We'll start electrolysis on it in an hour or so."

He bent and examined the other encrustation. Jesse leaned

over the tub beside him. A fine mist of bubbles was rising from many places in the clump and already, a number of flat disks were visible.

"Sure looks like coins to me," Russ said. "But what's that in the middle?"

All the detritus that had accumulated on the clump was dissolving and flaking away wherever the wrapped wire came in contact with it.

Russ bent closer, examining the partially dissolved cluster of coins from different angles.

"I really don't know," he said. "But look at the arrangement of the coins."

The largest part of the cluster had more than a dozen flat disks, which looked to be stacked haphazardly and crooked. The thing in the center was T-shaped and bulging on one side. A few disks had fallen away, but it was easy to see where they'd fallen from.

Jesse shuddered. "Was all that in some dead man's pocket?"

"Not exactly," Russ said. "Uniform trousers of the time had large pockets in the side seams for tools of the trade. Most sailors kept their valuables in a leather pouch, tied around their neck or waist."

"That's a crucifix," Jesse said. "He was a Huguenot."

Russ looked up at him. "Isn't that French?"

Jesse nodded. "A lot of French Huguenots settled in England in the fourteenth and fifteenth centuries. This probably also puts the wreck at after 1680."

"Why's that?" Russ asked, using a small metal pick to chip away obvious detritus.

"Huguenots, or French Protestants, migrated to England in

waves to avoid persecution in France, which was predominantly Catholic," Jesse replied, looking closer at the middle part. "The second wave was in 1680, when King Louis XIV revoked a royal decree that had protected them in France for a century.

"The first wave was a hundred years earlier," Jesse continued. "And those Huguenots would probably have assimilated into English Protestant culture over four or five generations. English Protestants wore crosses, not crucifixes."

Russ put the pick down and stared at Jesse. "Someone paid a little too much attention in World Religion 101."

"Don't mock," Suzanne admonished him. "I love historical stories, Jesse."

"Hymie has a photographic memory," Rusty said, leaning over Russ's shoulder. "Is that a mint mark?"

Russ looked down at the coins on the bottom. He picked one up and gently toweled it off, then placed it on a black rubber mat beside the tub.

Suzanne opened a drawer on the other side of the room and brought Russ a large magnifying glass. He bent over the coin and studied it carefully.

"It is," he finally said. "It looks like 1714."

"What's that mean?" Rusty asked.

"It means you probably found the lost Dutch Guineaman," Suzanne replied.

"Guineaman?" Jesse asked. "Because it carried gold coins?"

Russ shook his head. "A Guineaman specialized in carrying *human* cargo."

"Slaves?"

"Yes," Suzanne replied. "Teach captured it off St. Vincent in

1717, killed the French crew, and released the surviving Africans on the beach."

"That was the ship that'd been dispatched to Virginia for supplies," Russ added. "They almost made it back."

"How many crew?" Rusty asked solemnly.

"Over a hundred," Suzanne replied. "It was the ship William Howard commanded before he retired in the summer of 1718."

Russ nodded. "His second officer commanded the Guineaman on the supply run."

"So this ship probably sank between then and when Teach was killed the following November," Rusty said. "But what would a French Huguenot be doin' on one of Blackbeard's ships with English coins in his pouch?"

"Pirates didn't care what the nationality was of a coin or a sailor," Russ said. "An able-bodied seaman was measured by his ability, not his religion. In far-flung lands, a coin was worth what it weighed. I've heard of treasure finds that had Spanish coins mixed in with French, English, and Dutch."

Suddenly, there was a roaring sound just over the roof of the shop that droned away toward the east.

"That should be your grandfather," Suzanne said, then turned to Russ. "Take the Jeep. You haven't driven it in a week."

"Let that soak," he told her, then looked down at his son. "Want to go for a ride in the Jeep?"

The boy smiled. "Jeep! Wanna ride the Jeep!"

Chapter
Twenty-One

◆━━━━◆━━━━◆━━━━◆

J esse sat up front, while Rusty and Russ's kid took the narrow backseat, tucked between the wheel wells. When Russ started the engine, it sprang to life instantly and settled into a quiet rumble.

Rusty grabbed both seat backs and hauled himself forward. "This buggy's got a V-8?"

"Those side pipes aren't for show," Russ replied. "It's got an American Motors 304 under the hood."

Russ backed out of the angled spot, then turned the Jeep tightly around the circle. It responded a lot like the M-151 military jeeps, quick and nimble, though obviously a good bit heavier, with more power, and bigger tires.

"The term jeep," Russ explained, "and later the *name*, came from the vehicle's nomenclature when it made its first appearance in the Second World War. It was classified as a lightweight general purpose vehicle, or 'GP' for short. It didn't take troops long for that to morph into jeep."

Russ shifted up through the gears smoothly as the Jeep

rumbled down the crushed shell road, rolling slightly as the tires and suspension absorbed the bumps.

When they reached the paved road, Russ turned right, and the tires started humming on the concrete like a herd of centipedes at double-time.

It only took a few minutes to reach the airport, where Russ bypassed the main building and pulled out onto the flight line. There were only two planes tied down there, a small single-engine and a slightly larger twin-engine.

"There it is," Rusty said, pointing toward the setting sun.

Jesse stood up in the Jeep and turned around, holding onto the rollbar as he waved. The plane was already on the runway, not even halfway along it, and was slowly taxiing toward them.

Russ parked in front of the single-engine, high-winged plane, and jumped out, looking down the runway.

"Nice plane," he said, pulling a ballcap over his head to block the setting sun. "What is it?"

"That's a *radial* engine," Rusty said, standing up in back with Russel Junior. "No idea what kinda plane, though."

It was big. Bigger than the airplane they were parked next to, which looked like it couldn't hold more than four people who'd be very tightly packed inside.

The approaching plane was also a high-winged, single engine, but even at a distance, Jesse could tell it could probably carry quite a few more people, or even cargo. It had two over-sized front tires and a tiny rear one on a swivel, commonly called a taildragger.

But it was the wings that really set it apart. They looked far larger than even those on the twin-engine plane parked next to the one beside them.

"Look at the size of those tires," Russ said. "It's some kind of bush plane, probably built for taking off and landing on a short field or pasture."

Russel Junior covered his ears as the plane pulled into the next spot on the flight line, but his expression was one of pure joy.

The engine stopped, and after a moment, the door on the right side opened.

"Hey, Jesse!" Pap called out, as he climbed out onto a small step on the landing gear's main strut.

He dropped lightly to the ground as Jesse led the others toward the plane.

"Pap!" he said, embracing his grandfather tightly.

Jesse suddenly wished he'd just gone home instead, so they could sit out back by the river, fishing and playing fetch with Molly as they watched the sun go down. That's what old men did. Pap was sixty-three and retired.

"It's so good to see you," Pap said, releasing him.

"I'm really glad you came," Jesse said and turned to the others. "You remember Rusty, from Parris Island. And this is our squad leader… er, *former* squad leader, Sergeant Russ Livingston, and his son, Russel Junior. Russ is on leave here with his family before shipping off to Okinawa."

"Just Russ is fine, sir," he said, extending a hand.

Pap looked around, then shook his hand. "When someone calls me sir, I get the feeling my dad's around. Just Frank. I was an enlisted ground-pounder just like you."

Pap shook hands with Rusty. "Good to see you again, too. How are Shorty and Dreama?"

Rusty looked surprised. "They're just fine. Thanks."

Pap dropped into a full squat and looked at the boy. "Would you like to see my friend's airplane, young man?"

He pointed. "Airplane!"

"Come on," Pap said, rising to his full six-one. "I want you to meet someone."

They followed him around the front of the plane, where the pilot was just climbing down.

"Jesse," Pap said, "This is my friend, Henry Patterson. Henry, meet my grandson, Jesse, and his friends, Rusty, Russ, and Russ, Junior."

They exchanged handshakes and Henry immediately lifted the boy up into the pilot's seat, then stepped up onto the strut and helped him to stand up in the seat.

"This here's a 1954 deHavilland DHC-2 Beaver," he said to the smiling boy. "All you gotta remember is *Beaver*, though. Any pilot'll know what you mean."

"Henry and I met in the South Pacific," Pap explained to Russ and Rusty. "We were together on Peleliu, Iwo Jima, and Okinawa."

The pilot glanced down and laughed, then pointed at Russel Junior, who had both hands on the wheel of the plane and was rocking it back and forth.

"The way he's sawin' that yoke," Henry said, "this little one looks like he might be a *Navy* aviator one day."

The men laughed. "Can you stay for dinner, Henry?" Russ asked. "It won't be any imposition. We were planning to take Jesse out to Howard's Pub for his birthday, and we have plenty of room at the house, if you'd like to stay over."

Henry looked down and smiled. "I *was* just gonna hang out here for a couple hours and talk to some pilots, till all the day flyers are out of the sky." Then he looked around. "Something tells me there won't be many here, though."

"You're welcome to stay," Russ offered.

"Then I accept," Henry said. "But don't be too surprised if I cut out once it's good and dark. I love flying at night."

After Henry locked up and tied down his plane, they all walked toward the Jeep, Russel Junior riding on his dad's shoulders between Rusty and the old flyer.

Pap chuckled as he and Jesse trailed behind them. "I remember you used to do that. You'd pull on your dad's ears to make him turn."

"Russ asked us to come up here diving with him before our last leave," Jesse said. "It started out just being a weekend thing, then—"

"You don't have to explain, Son," Pap said, looking over at him with an expression of warm pride. "You're a grown man now. Look at you! I bet you're every bit of two-twenty now." He paused and looked at Jesse with great joy, something Jesse had rarely seen. "Mam and I brought you up for exactly this, Jesse—to be a man able to live on your own, with your own kind, and do things and make decisions for yourself." He stopped when the others reached the Jeep and appraised the transportation. "We, uh… We succeeded. We're riding in that?"

Henry turned around and started laughing. "Ya know, Frank, I do believe this is some kinda omen."

"Not a *omen*," Russel Junior said, giggling. "Dis is a Jeep!"

"He's right, Hank," Pap said. "It's just a jeep."

Then they both started laughing.

Rusty looked the most confused. "I don't get it."

Henry took a deep breath. "It was how we met. We got into a fight over a jeep."

"And it wasn't even the right jeep to start with," Pap added. "I was on rest and refit in Melbourne, after Cape Gloucester. Henry was a newly arrived replacement, and we'd both checked jeeps out of the motor pool."

"The danged things all looked alike," Henry added. "And we kinda tussled a bit until a Navy officer corralled us, asked our units, then drove off in the jeep we were fightin' over."

"Turns out," Pap finished, "Henry was a corporal, assigned to my squad, and I hadn't met him yet."

"You fought on Cape Gloucester, Peleliu, Iwo Jima, *and* Okinawa?" Russ asked, his tone almost reverent.

"We did," Henry said. "And Frank here was on Guadalcanal too. I didn't get to his unit till after that. First Marines lead the way!"

Henry turned and grabbed the back rollbar, stepped up onto the rear tire and then climbed in back and sat down on the fender.

"Sorry," Pap said to Rusty as he mounted the other side. "You and the boy are the smallest; you get the jump seat."

The rest of them piled in and Russ started the engine. Jesse gave him a "slow" signal as he turned the Jeep around on the flight line.

He needn't have; the roads were smooth, and the speed limit low, all the way back to Russ's house. Still, Jesse didn't think the two old men should be jostled.

Chapter Twenty-Two

W hen they arrived back at Russ's house, Suzanne was in the side yard, hanging sheets on the clothesline. The wind around her billowed the damp linens into puffy sails.

Russel Junior started yelling about the airplane as soon as he saw her, so Pap and Henry bailed out almost before the Jeep stopped. Rusty lifted the boy over to Henry, and when he put him down, he made a beeline to his mother.

"You didn't tell me your pap was part of the Old Breed, Jesse," Russ whispered, as the two of them trailed after the others. "Guadalcanal, Cape Gloucester, Peleliu, Iwo Jima, *and* Okinawa? Those were some of the toughest campaigns in Marine Corps history."

"I know that now," Jesse said with a shrug. "But growing up, he hardly ever talked about it."

Henry was shaking hands with Suzanne, who was smiling brightly as Russ announced that Henry was going to stay the night.

If she felt any burden, it didn't show.

"That'll be wonderful!" she exclaimed. "We have a rollaway bed we can put in Jesse's room."

"I'll take that," Rusty said. "Frank and Henry can bunk together."

"That's settled, then," she said, and turned to Russ. "The saltwater bath is almost finished. Why don't y'all go out to the barn and get the electrolysis started while I get the rollaway out. Natalie will be here in an hour and our reservation's at six."

"Electro what?" Henry asked.

"It's easier if I show you," Russ replied, looking at his watch. "But we'd best be quick."

"I'll be down in a minute," Suzanne said to Russ, then took the boy's hand. "But first I want to hear all about the airplane."

Russel Junior began chattering as they walked away, and the five men headed toward the backyard.

"I wasn't sure I flew over the right house," Henry said. "This is a heck of a spread for a sergeant."

"It's been in Suzanne's family for over two hundred years," Russ explained, as they walked toward the shop. "The whole island once belonged to one of her ancestors in colonial days."

"Is there some kinda offshore race going on here?" Henry asked, as they reached the door to the shop.

"Not that I know of," Russ replied. "Why?"

"We did a lazy turn out over the ocean to land upwind," he said. "Saw two racing boats out there running at high speed, headed south."

"Two?" Jesse asked. "One red and the other blue?"

Henry shook his head. "They had crazy paint jobs like some kinda abstract art, with neon colors. Hurt my eyes to look at 'em."

Four boats? Jesse thought, as they entered the shop. They couldn't *all* be smuggling drugs into the country.

"This isn't what I expected in a 'barn,'" Pap said, looking around as he entered.

"It was a barn in a past life," Russ replied, heading toward the two tubs with the silver clumps. "It's sort of a processing lab now. Jesse, Rusty, and I just returned from a profitable treasure dive."

Pap looked at Jesse. "You mentioned diving. But hunting for treasure?"

"We think Russ found the wreck of one of Edward Teach's pirate fleet," Rusty said. "That was Blackbeard's real name."

Russ reached behind the tank and opened a valve. Immediately, the water level began dropping, exposing the clump as he got the things he'd need to start the electrolysis, and then began to wind wire from a spool around the clump with practiced hands.

Rusty picked up one of the gold coins and showed it to Henry. "This here's the 1680 English guinea I found. So we know the wreck was after that."

Rusty moved to the other tub. "There was two possible ships that went down after 1680, Teach's supply ship in 1718 and an English warship." He pointed at the other tub, now with four coins resting on the bottom. "At least one of these pieces of silver is a 1714 English coin. So the wreck was obviously after *that* date too." He pointed to the middle of the clump and nodded at Jesse. "Accordin' to Jesse, that's a crucifix in the middle, and he's sayin' the sailor who owned it was a Frenchman."

Henry nodded. "A mass pilgrimage to England, also in the

late 17th century, I believe. But a Frenchman on an English pirate's ship, wrecked on the coast of America?"

"I think it adds more weight to it being a pirate ship," Jesse said. "Russ found those yesterday, along with more 1680 guineas. But like Rusty said, the 1714 coins rule out the English warship."

"Unless the two ships wrecked in the same place," Pap said, which caused Russ to pause his mixing to look over at him.

"I hadn't even thought of that," Russ said.

"Like in *The Deep*," Rusty added. "That movie with Jacqueline Bisset."

"The novel was better," Pap commented, as he bent to study the coins closely. "Though the movie did have some damned perky moments."

Jesse's mouth fell open and his face drained. He hadn't seen the movie, but the posters in some of the guys' wall lockers and the ads on late-night TV couldn't be missed.

Had Pap seen the movie? Seen the actress's practically bare breasts?

The man had never made a crude remark that Jesse knew of. He'd never seen him even glance at another woman, and he rarely uttered a curse word, unless a tool slipped in his grip, and he bashed a knuckle.

Nor had he ever been as outgoing and jovial as he'd been since he and Henry landed, Jesse thought. They'd both laughed and played with Russel Junior on the drive back.

Pap had always been serious and level-headed, always planning and working on goals, mostly for Jesse. He told jokes on occasion, but nothing crude, and he never joked about anything in public.

It was Henry's place on Andros Island that Jesse and Rusty

had gone to after the run-in with Bear Bering, though Henry wasn't there at the time; he'd been in Nassau, looking at a boat. When Pap had suggested it, he'd told him that he'd stayed there several times on fishing trips.

Jesse glanced at the others.

Pap was with *his* own kind again—Henry and Russ, both combat veterans. That was why he was acting a little differently. He probably felt more comfortable.

With sudden awareness, Jesse realized that *he* was also a part of it now—the Marine brotherhood.

His grandfather, by virtue of being a Marine, was also his brother, in a way that real siblings couldn't understand.

He felt that Pap knew this as well.

The sound of a car in the driveway got Russ's attention, and he started for the door. "That'll be my buyer," he said. "Be right back."

"Buyer?" Henry asked.

"He's got a guy who's gonna buy up all these gold guineas."

"Except the one you're keeping for your share," Jesse said. "From today's dive."

Rusty shrugged. "I decided not. Me and Jewels are savin' up every nickel we can."

A moment later, Russ returned with a guy carrying a brief-case, who looked like he should've been in an accounting office somewhere, except for his clothes. He wore faded jeans and a white T-shirt. He was balding, wore glasses, and needed to spend some time in the sun doing something.

"I've got twelve guineas," Russ told the man as they came in. "All dated 1680, but only eleven are available."

Rusty waved both hands. "No, no, they're all available."

Russ glanced over at him. "I thought you were—"

"Changed my mind."

"Okay," Russ said, turning back to the man. "A dozen."

The man peered in the older of the two trays holding clumps of silver coins. "Any idea what the silver is yet?"

"Only two are clearly identifiable so far," Russ said, both 1714 English shillings."

He looked at the newer clump. "Is that a cross in with these?"

"A crucifix," Jesse said. "Or at least I think so."

He bent closer, examining it through the water. "Oh, I'd be very interested in that. As well as the gold chain and whatever pendant it has on it."

"My wife's going to keep the necklace," Russ said.

"I'm not interested in silver after Charles's reign," the man said. "But if the cross can be removed now, I'll pay you five hundred for it."

Russ's expression remained neutral, not giving away anything he was thinking. "As far as the crucifix goes, can you come back in a couple of days? It's not ready to be separated yet."

He placed his case on an empty spot on the counter and opened it to withdraw a checkbook and pen. "Make it out to your wife, same as before?"

Russ nodded, and the man quickly made the check out and tore it from the little booklet. "Nine thousand even," he said, and handed it to Russ. "Consider the extra six hundred a deposit on the cross."

He took the check, looked at it briefly, then stuffed it in his pocket as the man put the checkbook away and removed a small lock box.

Russ unlocked another drawer and removed more coins, putting them in the man's box. Then together, they removed the ones that were still in the water and toweled them off before adding them with the others.

The man put the little box in the briefcase, closed it, and spun the little wheel codes on the front.

"Something tells me there might be more," he said to Russ. "Do you know what you've found yet?"

Russ waved a hand toward the door. "Not exactly. I may know more later this week though."

"Call me when you know about the cross," the bean counter said.

"You can bet on it," Russ replied, and closed the door.

"He sounded like he really wants that crucifix and necklace," Henry said, after Russ closed the door.

"That's the main reason I stalled him," Russ said without turning around. "I picked up on his interest too and have no idea what either one is worth."

Chapter Twenty-Three

◆ ◆ ◆ ◆

They'd spent the day diving, something each of them had done countless days with other friends. But on this day, the three of them had found *treasure* together, and now they'd been paid for it.

A lot.

Russ turned around slowly as he pulled the check from his pocket and held it up, grinning. "This is more than I earn in a year as a sergeant."

"Nine grand?" Rusty asked in disbelief. "For just two days of divin'?"

He laughed. "Those other four from the drawer were from a dozen previous dives. Not to mention research and just plain hunting before I found the first one. But now…" He paused and looked at Jesse and Rusty. "Now, we're zeroing in. And I leave in two weeks."

"Why was he so insistent on calling it a cross instead of a crucifix?" Jesse asked. "It's obviously a cross with *something* on the front of it, obviously depicting the crucifixion."

"I'm not sure," Russ replied, then gazed out the window for a moment. "But he does seem highly interested." Then he turned back to the others. "We'd best get up to the house and get ready for dinner."

An hour later, with the babysitter and Russel Junior perched in front of the TV watching *The Wonderful World of Disney*, the six of them piled into Suzanne's big Bonneville, which Russ drove, while Suzanne sat in the middle, next to Jesse, on the spacious front bench seat.

"Enough room back there?" she asked over her shoulder.

"More than enough," Pap replied, as Jesse glanced back.

Rusty was in the middle, but with none of the three men even close to being called large, there was plenty of shoulder room in the big, four-door sedan.

"You said this place is called Howard's Pub?" Henry asked. "And your maiden name is Howard? Are you related?"

"The owner's like a sixth or seventh cousin," Suzanne replied, as Russ turned out of the driveway. "At least one person from every generation has remained here in the Outer Banks since the early 1700s. I have over thirty cousins here. Probably more."

When they arrived at the restaurant, Jesse noticed the large deck with a view of the beach not far away. When he looked back toward town and across the marsh, he could see the masts of sailboats in the bay.

There were maybe ten people in the main dining area, mostly couples, and the hostess led them upstairs to a round table situated under the overhang of a roof that only covered half the rooftop dining area.

There were a few more people there than in the main dining

room below, and the view was the reason. In one direction was the Atlantic and an almost untouched wild shoreline, and in the other, the quaint little village surrounding the bay, and Ocracoke Sound beyond it.

Their table was easily large enough for ten people, but chairs had been removed, and everyone had plenty of space.

"How old is this place?" Jesse asked, looking around at what appeared to be a throwback to early sailing days.

"In two weeks, it'll be a year since the grand opening," Suzanne replied taking a seat.

The men all sat as one, and Jesse looked around again. "I don't know why, but I assumed it was older."

She smiled. "That's just what Ron wanted visitors to feel. When he opened last year, it was the first time in half a century that alcohol was served on the island."

"Prohibition?" Rusty asked.

"That's what closed the last bar," Russ said. "But until recently, nobody's been interested in opening one or going to one."

"Tourism is finally making its way out here," a man said, approaching the table. "Hello, Suzanne, Russ. And you've brought friends."

She and Russ rose and the man exchanged a quick hug with Suzanne, then shook Russ's hand.

"Ron, these are my friends," Russ said. "Frank, Henry, Jesse, and Rusty. All fellow Marines."

His eyes widened as he looked around. "Ah, the Marines have landed! Welcome, gentlemen."

Just beyond the bar owner, Jesse noticed a large trawler

maneuvering into the small bay. It was nearly a mile away, but it looked like several people were on the flybridge.

A young woman approached their table, and Ron waved a hand toward her. "This is Joyce; she'll be taking care of you. Again, thank you for coming. But I need to return to the kitchen."

The waitress told them about the catch of the day and took their drink orders. Though nobody had asked for an ID, Jesse ordered iced tea, while everyone else ordered beer, wine, and spirits.

Over Rusty's shoulder, Jesse could see the big trawler slowly moving toward the marina, then it stopped and turned around–practically within its own length– before backing into a slip.

He assumed the ease with which it was done meant the boat probably had two engines, or a very skilled driver.

Probably both.

The waitress returned with a tray full of drinks, and once she'd passed them around, Russ stood.

"A toast," he said, raising his glass.

Everyone stood with him.

Russ tipped his glass toward Pap and Henry. "To the Old Breed in our midst," he said, almost reverently. "And to their brothers, who didn't make it home."

"To the *New* Breed," Pap said, raising his glass. "May your bond in peace be as great."

Jesse knew that Pap had enlisted at twenty-five, much older than most privates, and he'd quickly moved up in rank. He also knew Pap had lost friends in battle. He'd fought in more campaigns than most Marines did during the war.

But he'd only recently learned his grandfather had been

wounded in action on Okinawa, his only injury in three-and-a-half years of fighting in the Pacific, and then he'd been medically retired as a gunnery sergeant at the end of the war.

"I feel like an outcast," Suzanne said, as they all sat back down. "In a bar owned by my cousin, on an island I was born on. Such an odd feeling."

Henry nodded toward Russ. "He's a sergeant, so I'm guessing he's deployed before?"

"He's going to Japan in two weeks," she replied. "The second deployment since we've been married. And he went to Vietnam before we met."

Henry smiled and sat back. "So you know how hard this comin' deployment's gonna be. You're not a normal wife, young lady. You're a *Marine* wife, so that makes you part of the *inside*, not an outsider."

Even from a distance, Jesse could see the men on the trawler seemed to be having a great time; all the boat's deck lights were coming on, as well as those inside the cabins. Light spilled out over the waters as music reached their ears.

Jesse felt a chill—a sort of tingling on the back of his neck. Shrugging his shoulders, he moved the collar of his shirt, then looked behind him and up at the ceiling, expecting to see a fan or something.

As he looked around the deck, his mind registered the number of people without his thinking. Several diners were watching the antics on the trawler just across the marsh.

Looking back at it, Jesse noted that one man in the group towered over the others. He stood on the uncovered back of the flybridge, looking out at the last of the sun's light to the west. He could literally turn around and look *over* the bimini top.

"You see that guy?" Rusty asked him, as he too eyed the trawler. "I bet he's taller'n you."

Pap's boatyard had all the manual tools to do just about anything, including a tubing bender, and his friends often came to him for replacement pieces of aluminum tubing when a bimini support broke. So Jesse had bent a lot of tubing for custom sun covers on boats, and he knew that a height of 76 inches was usually standard, just an inch over Jesse's six-foot-three.

"Way taller," Jesse said, quietly. "At least six-six."

Their food arrived, carried by the waitress and a young busboy, who was probably fourteen or fifteen.

Jesse grinned, remembering his very first *real* job. He'd done a lot of work for Pap and his friends, and many of them had even paid him, but the first time he went out to get a job on his own, he became a dishwasher and busboy at a local diner that was a short bike ride from Mam and Pap's house—The Gallie Ho.

He nodded politely to the kid—himself, just four years ago.

"It looks like Hal may have sold his boat," Suzanne said, looking across the marsh toward the marina. "That, or he found the money to keep it. Either way, it sure looks like someone's celebrating over there."

The tall man on the boat turned around, as if hearing her words. And when the wind whipped the hair back off his forehead, he looked familiar to Jesse.

Chapter Twenty-Four

———◆———◆———◆———◆———

The catch of the day was dolphinfish—also called mahi-mahi and dorado in other parts of the world—and Jesse had ordered his blackened, as did Rusty. It was excellent and had a serious bite to it.

"I've been to places where a man can eat like this every day," Henry said, smacking his lips. "Live in a thatched hut on the beach, get drunk every night, and not spend a regular working man's daily pay in a whole month."

Pap nodded in agreement. "Those places are becoming fewer," he said. "Especially in coastal areas. Fisheries are being overwhelmed by big commercial ships to feed the burgeoning population. The world's struggling to feed itself in some places."

"That's not a problem here," Suzanne said, smiling. "Our fishermen harvest for the locals and are good stewards of the sea. We've relied on it for centuries with little outside help."

Halfway through the meal, a man with long hair and a scraggly beard came up the outside steps and looked around. Jesse recognized him mostly by his clothes as one of the men partying on the trawler. He wore a bright, lime-green shirt with the sleeves cut off. After one look, he disappeared and ran back down to the boat.

Several minutes later, five men came up the outside steps, one being the guy who'd come up earlier, and another, the giant Jesse had seen on the trawler's flybridge.

The image of the racing boat they'd seen flying through the inlet into Pamlico Sound popped into Jesse's head, and he felt almost certain that the tall guy in the group was the one who'd been riding in back of the boat and had pointed at them on the dock.

The men headed straight to the bar, all laughing and talking at once, obviously well on their way toward an uproarious drunken celebration.

Pap stiffened as a shouted vulgarity reached their ears. He had his back to the bar, Henry on one side, and Rusty on the other.

The men at the bar got quiet as the bartender took their orders, then even louder once the drinks arrived.

One of the men, the long-haired one who'd come up moments before, spotted Jesse watching them and started toward them, stopping to say something to a young couple.

The girl's face flushed, and the young man started to get up, but she stopped him.

"How's that fish, old man?" Long-hair asked over Pap's shoulder.

Jesse tensed. Rusty and Pap were both between him and the drunk.

When he reached over Pap's shoulder to grab a piece from his plate, Pap smacked his hand.

"This is just what I was talking about," Pap said to Suzanne, across the table from him, ignoring the man standing behind him. "Too many people leads to having an overabundance of those who think they can just take and take without contributing anything."

The laughter and rough talk at the bar ceased.

"Then you get degenerates like these," Pap went on, loud enough for the men to hear. "Talking like drunken sailors on leave in Thailand with decent women and children in the room."

One corner of Henry's mouth curled upward, and he winked at Jesse.

"Who the fuck do you think you are, old—"

Pap was suddenly out of his seat, whirling so fast he caught the man completely off guard.

His right hand, hardened by decades of manual work, closed around the man's throat as Pap drove him backward with great force and slammed him up against a wall, dart boards on either side.

"You want to know who I am?" Pap hissed in the man's face, towering over him and leveraging himself against the man's throat with his full weight.

Henry was the first to move, but only by a fraction of a second, as three of the remaining four men at the bar started forward.

Pap spun with the long-haired guy and brought him down on his back onto a heavy oak table situated between the two groups of men.

His hand was still clutching the man's throat in a grip Jesse knew was as strong as a vice, even at his age.

One of the men, the cleanest looking of the bunch, pointed to Pap and said, "Moose."

The giant stepped forward, headed toward Pap, and before he even thought of it, Jesse snapped a side kick at the man's head as he got within range.

Jesse's foot connected with the side of the big man's face, and he toppled like a puppet with its strings cut.

Out of the corner of his eye, Jesse saw Suzanne step up beside Russ, pointing a small handgun at the men.

Pap looked up at the apparent leader. "My *name* is Frank McDermitt and that's my grandson, Jesse."

The guy in his grasp struggled and Pap tightened his grip. "That's *who* I am. *What* I am is the merciless, cold-hearted specter of your worst nightmares. I've fought better warriors than you punks in three different countries and *killed* them. Drag that cyclops out of here and leave us to eat in peace, or die right here, right now."

Around the room, Jesse heard the scraping of more chairs, and for a moment, he thought that these drunk guys were locals, and they now had Jesse and his friends sorely outnumbered.

"The gentleman speaks for all of us," a man behind Jesse said, much to his relief.

"We've had enough of your kind here," another voice added.

"We don't want any trouble," the leader of the group said warily, looking straight at Suzanne's gun. "Let Tim go, and we'll leave."

With a heave that belied his age, Pap grabbed the shirt of the man named Tim and sent him sprawling backward off the table. Then he pointed at the stairs and growled, "Go back to wherever you came from. Do it now!"

Long-hair scrambled to his feet, clutching at his throat, as the others, including the old man who'd remained at the bar, helped the giant to his feet and started down the steps.

Surprisingly, the drunk men staggered toward the parking lot beside the marina instead of going back to the boat.

Pap turned and pushed back his hair, which had fallen in his face during the scuffle. "I think we were talking about Outer Banks fishing."

Chapter Twenty-Five

◆ ◆ ◆ ◆ ◆

Everyone was talking at once as they returned to their table and sat down. A few of the other patrons came over and shook Pap's hand. One man even offered to pay for his meal, but Pap politely declined.

The quickness with which he'd seen Pap react surprised Jesse. For quite a while, he'd been admonishing Mam to consciously slow herself down as they got older, and Jesse had seen Pap doing just that over the years, taking a full day to do a task he used to do before lunch.

Jesse had always known his grandfather was a *strong* man, both physically and morally, but now he was starting to see him differently.

Pap could be dangerous.

Jesse kept a watch on the road into town and after a few minutes, a car drove by with four men in it. One of the two in the backseat was obviously the big man he'd side-kicked. The guy in the front passenger seat was the leader, and he was looking up at the deck as the car rolled past.

"That guy was at least four inches taller'n you," Rusty said. "Six-seven if he's a foot."

Even in training, Jesse had never had a coach hold a focus mitt as high as he'd had to kick to connect with the guy's head, and he felt certain that was as high as he could possibly deliver a kick while keeping the other foot planted.

"Have you ever seen any of those guys before?" Russ asked Suzanne. "They definitely came from Hal Gray's boat."

"One's a local," she replied. "Roy Calhoun."

"Which one was he?" Jesse asked.

"The smaller one with the blond hair," she replied. "He's from Hatteras. The old man that came in with them is Charlie Noble. He's been here since last fall, living on his sailboat, docked at the marina. I've never seen the other three."

"Hatteras is north of here?" Jesse asked. "That's the way they drove off."

"That's the only way you *can* drive from here," Russ said. "What kind of car was it?"

"A dark blue Mercury Montego," Jesse replied. "A '73 or '74, I think. License number TND-365."

"You remember the tag number, but not sure on the year?" Russ asked.

Jesse shrugged. "I've never been that big into cars."

"I think that's what Roy drives," Suzanne said. "But I think it belongs to his dad."

Jesse turned to Russ. "The big guy they called Moose was on that racing boat we saw come through the inlet yesterday."

"Are you sure?" Russ asked.

"Pretty sure," he replied. "It was at a distance, but there aren't many people that big."

Ron appeared and, after the bartender explained what had happened, tore up Joyce's order ticket, refusing any attempt by Suzanne or Russ to pay for the meal.

"We've been having a few problems like that," Ron said. "Mostly from out-of-towners. But thank you, gentlemen, for putting a stop to them before anyone got hurt."

But two guys had *gotten hurt,* Jesse thought. The guy called Tim was nearly choked out, and the giant the leader had called Moose had probably been clocked harder than he'd ever been in his life.

Really big guys won fights by intimidation before the first punch was thrown. All a guy like Moose probably ever had to do was stand up. But big guys often didn't know *how* to fight. Moose would definitely fall into that category; he'd advanced on Pap as if none of the rest of them were any threat at all.

"I don't think that was a good idea," Jesse said to Pap, as the group started down the inside stairs. "You giving those men your name."

Pap looked over at him when they reached the first landing and winked. "I gave them *your* name, too."

"Neither of which was a good idea," Jesse insisted. "Those guys are probably dangerous."

"By identifying yourself," Pap began, "you are no longer an object to be bullied, but a person, and it conveys to your adversary that you don't fear reprisal. They won't come back."

Jesse grinned at his grandfather. "You kicked that guy's ass, Pap."

"The way I see it," Pap replied. "When someone starts in on an old man, it can't possibly turn out good for them."

"Why's that?" Rusty asked, standing on the step below the landing and listening.

"The younger man will become known as someone who beats up old people," Pap replied, as he started past Rusty. "Or he'll be remembered as the guy who *got* beat up by an old man. Neither is good street cred."

Street cred? Jesse thought.

He was seeing a whole new, very capable, side to his grandfather. One he'd never known. Pap was sixty-three years old, yet his reaction and strength during the altercation had seemed like that of a man half that age. Or even a third.

And he'd cooly controlled the situation the whole time.

Jesse figured he'd have to keep an eye on Pap later, when the adrenaline wore off. But right now, he was laughing and socializing as if nothing had happened.

Chapter
Twenty-Six

———◆—◆—◆—◆———

R ingo was both pissed off and elated at the same time. He was pissed that he'd let himself and his friends get out of control while they were still in the delivery area. Not a good idea when your only means of transportation was a racing boat that was easily recognizable.

Roy's grandpa, who was like a third cousin twice removed from Ringo, owned a piece of property on the outskirts of Hatteras with an actual boat house. It'd been built to house a thirty-two-foot cabin-cruiser, which probably no longer existed. But it hid the Cigarette from the road, at least. The back ten feet stuck out, but Roy had produced a large blue tarp to cover that.

Ringo was elated because he'd not only sealed the deal on the boat, but he'd recognized the chick with the gun. She was the same one who'd been on the crab boat they'd seen coming in. The one wearing the short, cutoff jeans.

In the backseat, Moose and Tim were quiet as Roy drove past the restaurant they'd just been thrown out of. Ringo looked up at the deck and could see the tall kid looking down at them.

Just as well, he thought.

They'd been slamming shots while on the sea trial, since he'd closed the deal with Hal Gray while just outside the jetty. Probably too much celebration. The last thing Ringo needed was the cops sniffing around when he was about to use drug money to buy what was basically an expeditionary yacht.

Gray had said that he had others coming to look at the boat on Monday, so Ringo had simply opened his briefcase and taken a bundle of hundred-dollar bills out and handed it to the man, telling him to cancel the showings and, as soon as he could arrange the title transfer, he'd get the rest of the money.

There was just something about being handed $10,000 in cash that made a person agreeable.

"I'm gonna kill that—"

"You're not going to do anything," Ringo shot over his shoulder at Moose. "I don't need any cops checking on this deal."

"He kicked me when I wasn't ready," Moose complained. Then his voice dropped to a growl. "And that girl pointed a gun at you, Ringo."

"Just let it go, man," Tim said. "Ringo's right. We went a little overboard with the tequila shots, man."

"At least Hal thinks he can get the paperwork done by Monday evening," Roy commented. "Like he said, most of it's done; he just needs

to wait for the bank to open to notarize things so he can do the title transfer."

Ringo was mulling things over with just that in mind. It was Saturday evening, and would likely be forty-eight hours, late

Monday, before he could take the trawler. And that was if everything fell right into place like dominos.

He felt like staying in the area, maybe scoping out the house where the blonde lived, see what time her husband came and went.

If they hung out at Roy's place until Monday, they could motor home in *both* boats, which would mean that Tim would drive the Cigarette alone, leaving himself and Moose to get the trawler down to Wilmington.

Or they could all jump in the Cigarette in the morning, be in Wilmington a couple of hours later, and have Janet drive them back on Monday to sign the papers and hand over the cash. That way, he'd have both Tim and Moose with him on the trawler. But no time to watch the blonde.

"How ya plannin' to get two boats to Wilmington?" Roy asked, obviously thinking the same thing.

"I think we're going to head south in the morning," Ringo said, feeling that was the best option just from a crew perspective. "Then we'll have a friend drive us back up here to get the trawler."

"I got a better idea," Roy said. "Hire me to drive your Cigarette back for ya."

"It really takes two people," Tim said. "Unless you know it really well. How about I take it home in the morning, and have Janet bring me back here in her car tomorrow afternoon?"

Roy was his cousin, and he trusted the guy, but Tim was right. If anyone was going to drive the racing boat solo, it'd be either himself or Tim. There was too much risk of over-revving the engines coming off a wave at too high a speed. Whenever they ran fast, Ringo drove, and Tim worked the throttles.

"I ain't doin' nothin' next week," Roy mumbled. "Just sayin'."

Tim returning in the Cigarette, then coming back was a fifty-fifty probability. He'd just as likely start drinking until Janet got off work and then they'd spend an hour in bed before falling asleep and slumbering through until noon. Ringo knew how persuasive she could be.

"That old man at the marina," Ringo said, looking over at Roy. "He knows the boat. Think he'd be available to help out?"

"He did offer," Roy said. "Me too. That'll be five of us, man."

Four, Ringo thought. He wasn't counting on Tim returning, but he might have a job for him and the Cigarette before he left.

Roy glanced over at Ringo. "Don't take this the wrong way, but I don't think it's a good idea for the Cigarette to be seen around here for long. Some kid drift fishin' in a canoe might get curious and tell his old man what he seen under the tarp."

"You're right," Ringo said, reaching a decision, then turning to face the two in the backseat. "We'll call the marina as soon as we get to Roy's and get someone to have Charlie Noble call me. If he's agreeable, you can head out later tonight, Tim, but—"

"Keep it under eighty," Tim said. "I ain't Moose, man. I'll probably keep it under thirty, so if any Coast Guard radar picks me up, it'll look like it's just a sport fishing boat or something. Let me get some coffee in me and I'll slip out under cover of dark."

"I know you'll be careful," Ringo said, looking at Moose and grinning. "But that wasn't it. I want you to do something on the way."

"The ferry boat's about to leave," Moose said.

The ferry that would take them into Pamlico Sound and around Hatteras Inlet was just loading the last car when they arrived and there was room on it for several more cars.

Roy ran inside and got the ticket, then came back out and drove onto the boat's deck. As they were getting out of the car, the ramp started rising and two crewmen were hauling in the lines.

Moose looked back at land and rubbed his jaw. "We're gonna need a bigger boat."

"Is he okay?" Roy asked.

"Ignore him," Ringo replied. "Why don't they just build a bridge over the inlet?"

"They did build one over Oregon Inlet," Roy replied. "That's the next inlet north of here. On a *good* day it's a bitch to get through without banging your boat into the fenders of the bridge pilings."

They all went up onto the front of the ferry for the long ride. A good outfielder could throw a baseball across the inlet, but the ferry had to go well out into Pamlico Sound to get around the treacherous sandbars on either side of the natural inlet.

Ringo couldn't get the picture out of his head. That girl in the bar was scarier than any of the five guys. The way her cold blue eyes fixed on his over the gun's barrel had both disturbed and excited him. If he'd moved, he felt sure she would have shot him dead, then gone home for a peaceful night's sleep.

Leaning closer to Moose, sitting beside him on the foredeck, Ringo kept his voice low. "How'd you like to come back here, Moose?"

The giant looked down at him. "That girl pointed a gun at you, Ringo." The corners of his mouth turned up, but the expression was menacingly evil. "It'd be good to take her for a long boat ride like last time." He thought for a second as he rubbed his chin. "And that punk who kicked me and the old man who choked Tim too. We could take them on a boat ride when we leave on Monday."

Moose liked taking people for boat rides. The Cigarette had seating for five, and at the end of the previous summer, Moose had befriended a couple of college girls on a weekend bender before they returned to class in Raleigh, offering them a high-speed boat ride.

The two women never made it to Raleigh.

"What was it you wanted me to do on the way back?" Tim asked.

Ringo leaned forward and looked over at Tim. "I want you to stop at that last house before the inlet, where we saw the crab boat." Then he slapped Moose on the shoulder. "If a safe and clear opportunity presents itself, we'll take that little blond bitch for a boat ride."

Tim's expression registered his surprise. "You want me to grab her?"

"Just hang out there through the night," Ringo replied. "Do what you do best, and if she's available for a ride, yeah." He rested his elbows on his knees as he turned his head toward Moose. "She was pretty, huh?"

Moose nodded and made a lustful sound of agreement.

"Kind of on the small side, though," Ringo said, knowing he was just adding fuel to a fire. "I like tall women."

Ringo knew Moose liked the pretty ones, but as dumb and

big as he was, girls were just never interested. He also seemed to prefer petite women, and the smaller the better.

Ringo also knew that when the brute finished with one, she wasn't so pretty anymore.

So maybe Moose could go second, Ringo thought. He preferred taller, but damn! She'd looked extra hot holding that gun.

Chapter Twenty-Seven

———◆———◆———◆———◆———

T here wasn't much talk on the way back to Russ and Suzanne's house, and when they arrived, Suzanne went inside to check on the boy while the men walked around the side to the backyard.

Jesse liked the lifestyle of the small community, where people spent more time outside than inside, though he was sure the summers in the Outer Banks were probably just as hot as back home, and the winters a whole lot colder.

But at that time of year—mid-March—the weather was perfect for spending relaxing evenings outside.

Rusty headed straight for the shop out back to get the bottle of rum as Jesse walked with Pap and Henry, following Russ across the patio to where a fire ring was already set up with kindling and logs.

After a shot of lighter fluid at the base, the fire was lit, and the dry kindling began to pop and crackle as the fire grew quickly.

"I gotta say," Rusty said, sitting down next to Pap and

offering the bottle, "I was kinda surprised at how quick you moved back there at the restaurant. That dude never guessed he was dealin' with a bona fide badass."

To Jesse's surprise, Pap took the bottle and tilted the bottle to his lips. Then he used the back of his hand to wipe his mouth. "If it'd just been me and Norma," he said, as he passed the bottle to Henry, "I'd have just let that guy get away with it. I only acted because I knew you guys had my six."

"Don't let Frank's rather large size fool ya," Henry said to Rusty, then took a swig. "He looks big and clumsy, but I remember once, when a Japanese scouting party jumped our foxhole, I saw this guy go from a dead sleep to hand-to-hand fightin' in half a heartbeat."

"What happened?" Rusty asked.

"Why, Frank killed all four of 'em before me and Tate even got to our feet."

Jesse looked at his grandfather's profile as he began talking with Russ on the other side of the fire. His skin was now wrinkled and his hair gray, but he still had the same gentle face and demeanor Jesse remembered.

Pap glanced over for a second and in the firelight, Jesse imagined him as a much younger man, his utility uniform covered with blood and volcanic mud as he fought his way across the Pacific Ocean.

"But it was five against five," Rusty said. "Back there at the bar."

"Five *Marines*," Henry said, grinning and passing the bottle over to Jesse. "We had 'em outnumbered three to one."

Jesse tilted the bottle to his lips and felt the chilled rum burn the back of his throat as he swallowed.

The door to the kitchen opened and Suzanne came down the steps with Russel Junior and the babysitter, Natalie.

"Now that the excitement is over," Suzanne said, "it's time for this one to go to bed."

Natalie looked as if she was only a year or two younger than Jesse, probably still in high school. She was small and pretty, with straight dark blond hair, cut just above her shoulders. Her eyes were clear and so dark, he couldn't make out the irises behind oversized glasses.

Russ rose from his seat and pulled his wallet out, then handed the girl a ten-dollar bill. "Thanks for coming on short notice, Nat."

She pocketed the bill in her cutoffs and smiled. "I feel guilty accepting money to just watch TV and play with him. He's developing quite a personality."

Then she turned to Jesse. "Your name's Jesse, right?"

He nodded.

"There was a phone call for you," Natalie said. "A girl named Linda said she was sorry, but she wasn't going to be able to make it."

Jesse cut his eyes to Pap, then back to the girl, who was smiling at him. "Linda?"

Natalie nodded. "She said to tell you she was real sorry."

"That's too bad," Russ said, giving Jesse a knowing look. "I'm sure she had good reason."

She's fragile, he'd said. All the talk about her being the Ice Queen was bull. She was loyal, and now she was hurting.

"Walk me around to my car?" Natalie asked him.

Pap and Henry both grinned and shook their heads at one another.

"Sure," Jesse replied, then turned to Russ and the others. "I'll be right back." He waved at the little boy. "Goodnight, Russel Junior."

"G'night!" the kid called back as Jesse and Natalie started around the patio to the corner of the house.

"So, you're a Marine, like Mr. Livingston?"

He'd only known Russ for about six months and was just getting used to calling him by his first name, at his insistence, and only when off duty. To Jesse, he was *Sergeant* Livingston, not mister.

"Yeah," Jesse replied. "We're in the same unit. Or were. He's on leave before going to Japan for a year."

"I know," she said, as they turned the corner into the front yard. "It's going to be hard for Suzanne."

Jesse thought the difference in how she referred to the couple as Mr. Livington and Suzanne was a little odd.

"Suzanne told me what happened at Howard's Pub," she continued, then looked up at him. "She said you knocked a huge man out with one kick. Is that where you learned to fight? In the Marines?"

"Some," he replied. "I took martial arts for a few years before I joined." He spotted a small blue import. "Is that your car?"

"All mine," she replied. "I bought it used, with my babysitting money."

"Really?" Jesse said, genuinely impressed. The car didn't look like it was more than a few years old. "How long did that take to save up?"

"Well, I started when I was thirteen and I'm eighteen now, so five years. I just bought it last week."

"I'll be eighteen on Thursday," he said without thinking.

"No way!" she exclaimed, looking up at him. "I thought you were at least twenty-five. So… is this Linda your girlfriend?"

"Another Marine in our unit," Jesse replied. "We're friends, but not like boyfriend and girlfriend."

"How long are you staying with the Livingstons?"

"Rusty and I have to be back at the base a week from Monday," Jesse replied.

"Maybe I'll see you around," she suggested, opening the door and sliding into the seat. She closed the door and looked up at him through the open window, smiling again. "I have a car, so if you want someone to show you around…?"

She turned the key and there was a chattering sound under the hood.

"We're planning to do a lot of diving," Jesse said, as she tried to start the engine again. "But if it rains, I might have to take you up on that."

The chattering continued as she held the key over.

"Whoa!" Jesse said. "It sounds like the battery's dead."

Natalie looked at her watch. "Oh, great. I have to be home in fifteen minutes."

"Come on," he said, pulling her door open again. "I'll get Rusty's keys. He's got jumper cables in the trunk."

"That'll take too long," she protested, as she followed him around the house.

Suzanne had taken the boy upstairs and the men were talking around the small fire.

"Rusty," Jesse said, "Natalie's car won't start, and she has to be home in a few minutes. Gimme your keys."

"Take my Jeep," Russ said, standing and extending a set of

keys toward him. "It doesn't get much use." He paused a moment, as if a thought had just occurred to him. "In fact, I'd feel better if you kept it there on the base for me and use it while I'm gone."

Jesse's mouth fell open. "Wait… what?"

"I'll be coming back to Lejeune after Oki," he said. "You don't have wheels, and Suzanne will be out here and won't need it."

"I can't even *drive* it," Suzanne added, coming up behind them. "I never drove a straight drive before. And it'll be safer and better taken care of on the base."

"Here," Russ said, holding the key ring out on one finger. "Go. The clock's ticking." Then he folded the keys back into his fist. "You *can* drive a stick, right?"

"If it's got wheels or keels, he can drive it," Rusty said.

Jesse looked down at Natalie. "Leave your keys and we'll take a look at it when I get back." He turned and faced Russ, accepting the keys. "I'll take her home, then we can find out what's wrong with her car and fix it. But we'll talk about the rest later."

"Follow your last order first," Pap said. "Get moving."

Chapter Twenty-Eight

◆━━━◆━━━◆━━━◆

"Shotgun!" Natalie shouted as she ran toward the Jeep.

Jesse laughed, since it was only the two of them. He helped Natalie into the passenger seat, then went around and climbed in behind the wheel.

"This Jeep is *so* cool," she said, as he started the engine. "The perfect beach cruiser. You should take him up on his offer."

"I don't know," Jesse replied, turning on the headlights, then backing out of the spot. He shifted to first gear and let the clutch out a little too fast. The Jeep lurched as the big offroad tires dug a pair of gouges in the crushed gravel.

Jesse looked over at her and grinned. "Oops."

Natalie giggled. "*Yeah*, oops."

"You'll have to tell me where to turn," he said. "I don't know any street names around here."

"Left out of the driveway," she said. "Go half a mile and take the first right. What do you do in the Marines?"

"We're infantry," Jesse replied, then added, "The oldest guy there is my grandfather. He and his friend were Marine infantry too."

"But not your dad?"

Jesse nodded as he concentrated on shifting smoothly. "Dad was, too, but he was killed in Vietnam."

"Oh, crap! I'm so sorry. I didn't know."

He looked at her and smiled as he downshifted for the stop sign. "Don't worry about it. Of course you didn't. My mom and dad both died when I was eight. My grandparents raised me."

He made the right turn and drove slowly, waiting for her to tell him where to go next. Some people reacted differently than others when they learned he'd been orphaned as a boy. Others took it in stride, like Rusty.

"That can't have been easy," she said, looking ahead. "Take a right at the next stop sign."

"Mam and Pap made it as easy as it could have been," he said quietly. "They lost their only child and I was *his* only child."

When he reached the beach road and turned right, he was aware that the town was the other way. He shifted easily and accelerated slowly; there wasn't a lot of island left going that way.

"Do you see that sandy turn-off just up ahead on the right?" Natalie finally asked. "Turn off there."

Jesse slowed and turned into what he thought was a sand driveway, until the Jeep's headlights swept over a low dune with swift-moving water just beyond it.

He stopped and looked around. "Which way?"

"I lied," she said. "I'm eighteen and it's Saturday night. I don't have to be home."

"So... you—"

"Told a small lie to get you alone?" she replied, turning in her seat to face him, then removing her glasses and folding them into her lap. "Yes, I did, but I only intended it to be a ride home. Now I think I want to get to know you a little, instead of watching TV by myself."

"You didn't have to lie," Jesse said. "I'm sure we could have jumped the battery."

"Yeah, and that'd get me home," she said. "Then I'd have to get a neighbor to jump start it again tomorrow to go to church, then again after church... tonight wasn't the first time."

Jesse turned off the headlights and shut off the engine.

"It's dark," she whispered, her voice only competing with the sound of the water flowing by.

"It'll be a new moon tomorrow," he replied. "Give it a minute. Your eyes will adjust, and the stars are bright."

In the darkness, he saw her smile and push a strand of hair behind one ear. "You don't have to go far from the village to be in total darkness at night."

Jesse looked around. Small waves could be heard washing onto a sandbar in the distance. "So, I take it this is the world-famous Ocracoke Inlet?"

She swung her legs out and jumped to the ground. "Come on. I want to show you something."

Following her toward the dune, Jesse considered why Linda had decided not to come, and more to the point, why she didn't wait until later next week to decide. They hadn't planned on her being there until the following weekend anyway.

Natalie jogged out onto the shore side of the low dune. It wasn't wide, less than thirty feet to the water, but it got much wider as it wrapped around the back side of the island.

"Look," Natalie said, pointing out into the water just beyond the curve of the beach. "Do you see it?"

Jesse scanned the sandbar but saw nothing more than the remnants of a fallen dock or something. "Old pier posts?"

"It's what's left of a ship," she said, then pointed farther out into the darkness of the sound. "A side-wheeler that ran aground on a sandbar way out there more than fifty years ago. The whole sandbar has moved nearly a quarter mile since then, with the hull riding it like a surfer."

He could see it now. What he'd mistaken for posts leaning out away from each other were the thick, heavy rib timbers of an old wooden ship.

"A quarter mile in fifty years?" Jesse asked, scanning the water. "At that rate, it'll be right here on the beach by the year 2000."

"That's a long way off," she said, taking his hand and pulling him along the beach. "Follow me."

After forty or fifty yards, the dune flattened out, and beyond it was a pool of water.

"It's low tide," Natalie said. "This tidal pool's been here twice a day since I was little. It's where I learned to swim."

"You've lived here all your life?" Jesse asked.

She laughed as she waded into the calm water of the pool. It seemed to glow with a faint light around her ankles.

"As far as I know, only one person has ever moved *to* Ocracoke," she replied, looking down at her feet. "Almost everyone here can't wait to move *away*. Do you see this?"

"Some kind of bioluminescence or something," he replied, kicking off his flip flops and then wading out to her. His feet also seemed to glow on the sandy bottom. "I've read about this. Pretty cool."

"It's my nighttime magic place," she said, turning toward him.

Without warning, she stepped into his embrace, wrapping her arms around his back and pulling him down to kiss her lips.

"There," she said, stepping back. "We got that out of the way."

Jesse laughed at her impulsiveness. "So, you learned how to swim here? It's only a few inches deep."

"It's deeper when the tide comes in," she whispered, a slightly sad tone to her voice as she slowly moved her feet around, creating little swirls of light. "My mom and dad used to bring me here when I was little. Dad always told me it was the water fairies."

"What do they do?" Jesse asked. "Your parents."

She turned her head up to face him and he saw the light from a million stars reflected in her dark eyes.

"They died in a car wreck last summer," she said, lifting her chin defiantly. "I live with my aunt and uncle now."

Chapter
Twenty-Nine

$\blacklozenge$ — $\blacklozenge$ — $\blacklozenge$ — $\blacklozenge$

After Jesse dropped Natalie off at her aunt's place in town, he drove the Jeep slowly on the now-familiar roads back toward Russ's house. He had several thoughts swirling through his head and was in no hurry.

He liked Linda a lot, and what Russ had told him could easily explain why she'd canceled. Her boyfriend had died recently, and she was probably confused and afraid to get involved again so soon.

He could understand that.

Natalie had moved in with her mother's sister and her husband immediately after the wreck that had claimed her parents lives but wasn't really sure how much longer she'd stay. He could tell by the way she spoke of her parents that they were very close, and like him, she was an only child.

She'd asked if she could go out on the boat with them the next time they went, and Jesse told her he'd ask Russ. She'd scrounged a piece of paper and the stub of a pencil from the

Jeep's glove box, written her number on it, and asked him to call her in the morning, either way.

Jesse's thoughts turned to the men in the bar earlier. The one who'd picked on Pap—the guy the leader had called Tim—had looked like a degenerate. And though he was much younger—probably half Pap's age—the old man had a few inches in height over him, and at least forty more pounds of muscle.

Then there was the new-to-him knowledge that Pap had killed at least four men with his bare hands. An unknown factor to Tim, but one that Jesse was sure Pap thought of every day.

The leader had sounded well-spoken and was neatly dressed, at complete odds with his companions. Jesse had noted an expensive watch on his wrist and a heavy gold ring on his right hand. The racing boat probably belonged to him.

Remembering the night before, Jesse pictured the racing boat in his mind as it came roaring through the inlet. The guy in the back had looked over and pointed at them on the dock, and Jesse felt certain it was the same guy he'd kicked, the one they'd called Moose.

When he turned into the driveway at Howard House, he followed it to the circle and parked the Jeep where he'd found it, then climbed out and walked around the house to find everyone sitting around the fire.

"Back so soon?" Henry asked with a chuckle.

"It wasn't far," Jesse replied, extending the keys to Russ. "Thanks."

"You're welcome any time," Russ replied. "And I really hope you'll take me up on the offer. Leaving it sit for a whole year will ruin it."

"He's right," Rusty said. "Nothin' worse for a motor than sittin' for a long time."

When Jesse sat down, he heard a thumping sound.

Suzanne picked up what looked like a transistor radio and held it to her ear. "He's out of bed," she said to Russ, getting to her feet and handing the device to him. "I'll go put him back to bed, then I think I'm going to turn in myself. Good night, gentlemen."

They all rose and said goodnight back, then sat again as she started up the steps.

"What's that?" Rusty asked. "Some kinda radio?"

"It's a baby monitor," Russ replied, putting it back on the table beside him, his wife's soft voice coming over the speaker. "Basically, a cute walkie-talkie, with one being just a transmitter and the other just a receiver."

"Radar, satellite navigation, baby monitors..." Rusty said. "You do like your gadgets, huh?"

"No different than a Marine and his rifle," Russ replied. "It's a tool that gets the job done, but not absolutely necessary. I like to stay current with the times." He turned toward Jesse. "Nat's a nice girl, huh?"

Jesse nodded. "At first I thought she was just a kid, but she's older than she looks." Then he turned to Rusty and asked, "You saw the big guy on the back of that racing boat when it came through the inlet, right?"

Rusty nodded. "We were just talkin' 'bout that. I'm pretty sure you're right. He was the same guy at the bar you drop-kicked into next week."

"It was a planted side kick," Pap said. "Jesse's been taking martial arts classes since he was about six. Norma and I went to all his matches, and I've never seen anyone kick that high before."

"Hurt my groin, just watchin," Rusty added. "Head too."

"That'd explain why we never saw or heard them leave last night," Russ said.

"They didn't leave," Jesse said.

"And apparently," Russ went on, "one of them was interested enough in Hal's boat that he took them out for a ride."

"That big trawler?" Rusty asked. "If what you say is true, it wouldn't make sense, them usin' somethin' like that for what they're doin'."

"The Coast Guard can't catch them?" Henry asked. "In these go-fast boats they use?"

Russ shook his head. "There's half a dozen freighters a day go by here. They ride the Gulf Stream, which comes really close to Diamond Shoal, just a few miles offshore. Chesapeake Bay's just 130 miles up the coast, then New York is just beyond that. The Outer Banks are a choke point for commercial ships. The fast boats aren't from around here and it's doubtful they'd have the range for a long drug haul. So, everyone assumes they come from somewhere a little south of here and intercept the freighters way out in international waters."

"A boat like the one we saw," Rusty began, "could cover ten miles in the time it'd take a cutter to start the engines and throw off the lines."

"You said you live in The Bahamas, Henry," Russ said, changing the subject. "Which island?"

"I got a little place on the northeast side of Andros Island," Henry replied. "A tiny marina, blasted out of the limestone bedrock a century ago, that's big enough for six or eight boats. So far, I've built three little cabins on the shore there."

"I've never been to The Bahamas," Russ said. "What do you plan to do with this place?"

"Scuba diving tourists," Henry replied. "I plan to have six cabins, plus my old house, which is original to the property. Folks can come and rent the cabins real cheap, then rent or charter my boats to go out to the TOTO."

"Toto?" Russ asked. "Like Dorothy's dog?"

"It's short for Tongue of the Ocean," Pap replied. "A deep-water basin over a hundred miles long, surrounded by the Bahama Banks."

Russ sat forward. "How deep?"

"Over a mile," Rusty replied. "The Navy tests underwater acoustics there. Jesse and I stayed at Henry's place for a few days last summer, but he wasn't there. The drop-off is about a mile out and straight down."

"Natalie asked if she could go out on the boat with us," Jesse said, staring into the fire.

Russ grinned. "Just drove her home, huh?"

"We stopped down at the inlet," Jesse replied. "Just for a few minutes."

"Sure," he replied. "I knew her dad. She's good on a boat, as I recall."

"I'll be flyin' out early tomorrow," Henry said to Jesse. "You can drop me off when you go to pick her up."

Russ turned toward Pap. "You're coming out with us?"

"I'd love to," he replied. "But I'll just stay on the boat. My last dive was a few years ago."

Way out over the water, Jesse's ears picked up the faint sound of an engine burbling at low speed. The others heard it also, and they all looked out past the shop.

Suddenly, out beyond the sandbar, bright red and blue lights started flashing and a spotlight came on.

The sound of engines roared as the spotlight swept back and forth across the water.

"That's Andy Barret out there," Russ said, getting quickly to his feet.

"Who's he?" Jesse asked, standing and moving out into the yard with the others following.

"Deputy sheriff," Russ replied, just as the spotlight found what it was looking for.

"That's the same boat!" Rusty shouted.

Chapter Thirty

———◆———◆———◆———◆———

The two boats were so unevenly matched, the race was over before it even got started. Those on shore moved out into the yard, as the big blue racing boat, caught in the beam of the spotlight, rose up out of the water with the engines screaming. It was half a mile closer to the inlet than the police boat, already on plane, and headed toward the tip of the island and open water.

The pursuing sheriff's boat sped after it, but at almost half the blue boat's speed, there was no chance of catching it, and the drug boat, if that's what it was, disappeared through the inlet.

What was it doing sitting out there in the darkness? Jesse wondered.

Making a drug exchange? If they were smuggling in large quantities, like Russ believed, they wouldn't stick around to make small sales in clandestine locations in the middle of Pamlico Sound.

"There was only one person on board," Pap said. "Or the others were hunkered down."

"There was just one," Rusty agreed. "The light hit him just as he mashed the throttles and the bow came up. I could see the other seats clear as a bell."

"There were three when it came by here last night," Jesse said. "And there were four of them in the bar, plus the old man."

The police boat gave up, turning the lights off and turning around before even reaching the inlet.

"Suzanne said the other guy was a local," Russ reminded him, "from Hatteras. So two of the three who arrived are probably staying up there somewhere and only one is returning."

Henry turned to face the others. "That means the other two are goin' back to wherever home is by a different way."

"The trawler?" Pap asked.

"How well do you know the guy who owns it?" Jesse asked, glancing over at Russ. "Can you call him? Find out who the guy is who wants to buy it?"

"I can have Suze call him in the morning," Russ replied. "I'm as much an outsider here as any of you."

"He's comin' this way," Rusty said, pointing toward the long pier.

Russ picked up the baby monitor and held it to his ear as they all walked toward the water and the approaching police boat.

"Everything okay?" Jesse asked Russ.

"He's snoring," Russ said with a grin as he held up the little radio receiver. "And I don't hear the water running anymore, so Suze has probably gone to bed already. She always goes to bed early."

They walked out onto the pier and Russ and Pap caught the lines from the two deputies on the boat.

"Evenin', Russ," the older of the two said. "How's Suzanne and the boy?"

"She's fine," he replied. "And he's growing like a weed."

"Did ya see that blue boat a few minutes ago?"

"We heard it just a few seconds before you guys lit him up," Russ replied. "But we've seen the boat before."

"When was that?" the deputy asked.

"Near sundown last night," Russ replied. "They came through the inlet, running at least sixty miles an hour. Drug runners."

In the low light from the boat's instruments, Jesse saw the deputy smile. "Now, we don't know that for *sure*, Russ. Who else ya got here with ya?"

Introductions were made, and then the younger deputy, Clyde McCormick, asked Russ, "Are you sure you didn't see them out there earlier tonight?"

"Like he said," Pap concurred, "we heard the engine idling just before you turned your spotlight on."

"How'd you even know they were out there?" Rusty asked. "Ain't no moon tonight."

Jesse looked up at the boat's T-top. "Radar."

They stepped back and looked up at the radar array on the roof.

"When did you get that?" Russ asked.

"Just last month," Deputy Barret replied. "They were installed on two of our boats while we learned how to use it, then deployed this past week for the first time."

"Could you tell where that boat came *from*, Andy?" Russ asked.

"We spotted it an hour after sunset," he replied. "We were

off Cedar Island and headed to the dock for the evenin'. It came from somewhere up near Hatteras, and I thought the damned radar was messin' up. It was goin' fifty knots. At night."

"That was an hour after sunset?" Jesse asked, grabbing Rusty's wrist and turning it so he could see his watch. "Three hours ago? I thought Hatteras was just a few miles away."

The younger deputy pointed out into the darkness of the sound. "He was stopped out there for more'n two hours."

"It struck me odd that a fast boat like that would stop to bottom fish at night," Andy said. "I thought maybe they broke down, so we headed toward it. I decided to be a little stealthy when we were close enough to see lights and he didn't have 'em on."

"Took us an hour to get as close as we did," the younger deputy added. "But even with radar, there ain't no way we'd catch somethin' like that. As fast as that thing is, it'd be out of radar range before we could clear the inlet."

"So, you didn't see that boat sitting out there for the last couple of hours?" Deputy Barret asked again.

Russ pointed toward the house. "We've been sitting out there by the fire for about that long. A boat can't go through the inlet that we can't hear from out there in the yard."

"Tide's flooding," Jesse said. "I just saw the current down at the inlet less than an hour ago." He paused and looked at Russ. "He had to be anchored out there. We'd have heard the engine if he was even idling into the current."

Russ looked up at him. "What would somebody be——"

"Where were you before here?" Deputy McCormick asked.

"At Howard's Pub," Russ replied. "We went for dinner and drinks afterward, and got back here around 2030, I think."

"Yeah," Jesse agreed. "Natalie said she had to be home by 2100."

The older deputy looked up from his notepad. "Natalie? Oh… she was babysittin' the kid?"

"Yes," Russ replied. "We came straight out here when Jesse here drove her home and have been sitting out here ever since."

Deputy Barret nodded. "It's likely that boat was already there before you got back." Then he turned toward Jesse. "Natalie's eighteen, graduates in a couple of months, and it's not a school night. She doesn't have a set curfew, and she's got her own car."

It surprised Jesse that the deputy knew Natalie so well.

"I think the battery's dead," he said. "So, I drove her home in Russ's Jeep, and we were going to check her car out this evening, before this happened."

He looked over at the other deputy. "Grab the toolbox, Clyde." Then he stepped up onto the pier. "I told her that car was a lemon. Only four years old, and priced half what a decent used Ford or Chevy'd be."

"Has the battery ever been replaced?" Rusty asked, as the group of men started for the foot of the pier. "Even a good one's only gonna last a few years."

"No idea," Andy grumbled. "Damned Japanese cars."

Jesse was completely confused at this point. Sure it was a small island and everyone knew one another, but for a cop to take time off his duties to fix a car was beyond odd.

"I'll get a drop light," Russ said, heading toward the shop.

When they reached the car, Jesse opened the door and found the hood latch release, then Andy lifted the hood and raised a little bar to hold it open.

"Can't even put springed hinges on the hood," he muttered, and removed a flashlight from his utility belt.

Rusty pulled a rag from his back pocket and rubbed away some of the grime from the battery's sticker. "Right here's your problem. The battery's original; four years old. Probably won't hold a charge."

Russ joined them and plugged the end of a long extension cord into a wall outlet on the front porch. He turned on the light at the other end and hung it from the hood. "How many amps is it?"

Rusty used the rag again to wipe away more crud. "Ha! Only five hundred."

"My lawnmower's more powerful," Andy scoffed, as the younger deputy, Clyde, removed a hydrometer from the toolbox.

He pulled the caps off the battery, then tested each cell and came to the same conclusion everyone assumed. "Two dead cells. This thing's toast."

"I have a new spare boat battery in the shop," Russ said. "It's eight hundred amps but looks like it'll fit."

"I'll get it back to ya tomorrow," Andy said. "Once I run over to the garage and get her a new one."

Huh? Jesse thought. *Who the heck is this guy?*

"No hurry," Russ replied. "Like I said, it's a backup, and the one in the boat's brand-new too."

Ten minutes later, Natalie's car was running, and the old battery was in the trunk.

"Take the boat on back to the dock," Andy said to Clyde. "I'll just drive home from here."

Up on the deck, the screen door slammed. "What's going on out here?" Suzanne called from the porch.

"Just getting Natalie's car running," Russ replied. "Go on back to bed. I'll be up in a few minutes."

"No need for you to go out of your way, Deputy," Jesse offered. "I can return her car in the morning when I pick her up. She's going out on the boat with us."

Deputy Barret cocked his head in a curious way. "You dropped her off at *my house*, son. That ain't too far out of my way."

Jesse stood dumbfounded as the deputy shook Russ's hand, then got into the car.

As they were walking back around the side of the house, Jesse glanced back at the taillights turning out of the driveway.

"'Jesse,' he began, imitating Russ's Philly accent. "This is Deputy Andy Barret, Natalie's *uncle*.' You could have thrown that little bit of information into the introduction!"

The others laughed.

"You just let me make a fool of myself," Jesse said. "How was I to know?"

Pap put a hand on his shoulder. "Remember me always telling you to listen for the unspoken knowledge? Never assume anything not known."

"That's a good rule to live by," Russ agreed, looking out over the water as the police boat idled away.

"I picked up on it, bro," Rusty said. "And I ain't the most intuitive guy on the planet. Not many cops'll buy a motorist a battery and put it in for 'em."

"Take my Jeep in the morning," Russ offered, handing Jesse the keys. "Andy'll need her to leave her car at his place so he can change the battery in the morning." He grinned. "Besides, OBX chicks dig Jeeps."

Chapter Thirty-One

———◆———◆———◆———◆———

R ingo smiled in a sadistic way as the little boat puttered slowly toward Silver Lake Bay. The house was visible, just off to the right, where "Annie Oakley" lived, the hot little blonde who was with the bunch of guys who'd gotten them tossed from the bar.

The sun was just coming up and all he could see was one light on in the sprawling house. The small outboard boat turned slightly, entering the bay, and Ringo lost sight of the house.

But the image of the little blonde's face over the muzzle of the gun she'd pointed at him was indelibly stamped into his mind.

"Your time's coming, sweetness," he mumbled.

"Wha'zat?" the kid driving the boat asked.

"Nothing," Ringo replied. "Just thinking out loud."

By a sheer stroke of luck, Hal Gray's brother-in-law was a yacht broker and a notary, and he'd agreed to handle all the paperwork for a small fee. He'd also agreed to meet them at the marina at sunrise on a Sunday and would mail all the other documents once everything was done.

The only trouble was that the ferry between the islands didn't start running until mid-morning, which was hardly an insurmountable problem on an island that had more boats than cars. For fifty dollars, Roy hired a friend to take them by boat, running slowly in the darkness with no lights.

Tim had called him at Roy's house from Cedar Key not long after midnight to say he'd struck out, and was going to wait there until morning to get gas. He'd had to use quite a bit.

That was unfortunate, but being a Saturday night, he guessed it should have been more difficult than the last two smash-and-grabs they'd done. But he had an idea, and it would involve the trawler, too.

He'd told Tim to head back to Ocracoke in the morning. He wanted one more shot at grabbing the bitch who'd had the audacity to point a gun at him. He was expecting Tim to call on the radio, on channel nine, and pretend to be a fishing boat, and he would tell him if the crab boat was there or out on the water.

If the husband was out on the boat, Tim could make the grab quickly, and they'd meet up out in the ocean.

Tim had protested at first, but Ringo'd offered him an extra hundred, and a second go with the girl, after Moose had subdued her a little.

He'd become very agreeable after that.

Hal and his brother-in-law were waiting aboard *Nauti Gull* when the little boat pulled up to the stern, along with the old sailor, Charlie Noble.

Ringo made a mental note to find something to use to scrape

the name off just as soon as they got the boat moving back toward Wilmington.

Charlie was waiting at the swim platform to catch the line Roy tossed to him, then he tied the little boat off.

"You came from Hatteras in this?" Charlie asked, as he pulled the small boat alongside so Ringo, Roy, and Moose could climb out.

"Ferry don't run 'til nine," Roy said. "And don't let the size and appearance fool ya. Kip's little boat can run all day and night."

The men ascended the steps as Kip backed away, introductions were made, and Ringo sat down with Hal and his brother-in-law, James, at the little table in the living room.

James had a briefcase open and several documents on the table beside it. "This won't take long at all," he said, watching Roy and Charlie walk on through the living room and up the steps to the raised pilothouse.

"Good," Ringo said, as he heard the engines start. "I'd like to get going as soon as we finish."

The big boat rocked slightly as it moved out of the small bay and into Pamlico Sound. It'd taken just a little over an hour to sign all the paperwork and turn over the cash for the boat. Then Hal had spent another hour with Ringo and Charlie, going over the maintenance records on the boat and inspecting the engine room.

Ringo sat on the bridge of his new boat, next to Charlie,

who was driving. The commanding view through the wide windshield was impressive.

Moose and Roy were pulling the fenders in and stowing them in round brackets attached to the rails on either side of the foredeck.

"So what's the *top* speed again?" he asked Charlie, as they passed the last marker and the old man turned south.

"She'll cruise a long way at six or seven knots," Charlie replied. "If ya run her wide open, you'll get a bit more speed, maybe nine or ten knots, max. But you'll burn three or four times as much fuel to cover the same distance."

Ringo glanced over at him. "How do you know so much about this boat?"

"Used to be a shipwright with American Marine, the company that built her," Charlie replied. "But this'n was built long after I left there."

"And if we did everything possible to go as *far* as possible without stopping, how far would that be, and how would you do it?"

"Hmm, a maximum range scenario, huh?" he asked, rubbing the stubble on his chin. "Discountin' current, I guess ya could alternate engines and run maybe five knots, maybe nine hundred RPM, and I'd bet she could make thirteen, maybe even fourteen hundred miles."

They rode in silence for a minute or two, while Charlie steered the boat toward the inlet. Ringo knew that with that kind of range, he could go just about anywhere.

"Ever been to the South Pacific, Charlie?" Ringo asked. "New Zealand?"

"When I was younger," he replied. "Way before the war, I

sailed on an eighty-foot schooner bound from California to Australia."

"Non-stop?" he asked, impressed.

Charlie laughed as Roy and Moose entered the pilothouse. "Oh, hell no! We stopped a *lot*; every chance we could, and we stayed as long as we could. Took us a whole seven months to get to Tonga."

"What do you think the longest part of that was?"

"It's called the Milk Run," Charlie replied. "From the west coast of Mexico, you could stop at the Galapagos Islands, the Marquesas, then the Tuamotus, the Society Islands, then on to New Zealand. None of them jumps is much over a thousand miles, and that was pretty much what we did back in thirty-one."

"You sailed across the whole Pacific in 1931?" Roy asked in disbelief. "They didn't even have radar then."

"Not all the way," Charlie replied. "We'd planned to go to Australia, but the owner ran her aground and she sank just inside the reef on the island of Tonga. But from there, New Zealand's just a little over a thousand miles." He turned toward Ringo. "That where you want to take this boat? New Zealand?"

"I want to take it all the way around the world," Ringo replied, as the radio above their heads crackled.

The boat actually had four radios, two regular VHF marine band units, a battery-powered one, and a single sideband radio that could be used to receive weather information.

Ringo had already switched one of the VHFs to channel nine and that was the one crackling with static.

"Blue Bell calling Surf Rider," came Tim's voice over the speaker.

Ringo reached up and took the mic, giving the old man a

wink. He pressed the button on the side and said, "This is Surf Rider. Where are you?"

"About two miles outside the inlet," Tim replied, his voice getting clearer.

"There he is!" Moose exclaimed, pointing. "He's gonna need a bigger boat."

Charlie looked over at the giant with a puzzled look but said nothing.

"Slow down and let him get close," Ringo said, taking the battery-powered radio and heading out the side door.

Ringo moved toward the front of the trawler. His Cigarette boat was approaching, and Tim slowed, seeing him on the foredeck.

Pulling the underpowered handheld radio's antenna out, he waved the radio over his head until Tim did the same with the one they kept aboard the racing boat.

Ringo pushed the button on the side of the radio and held it up close to his mouth. "Can you hear me, Tim?"

"Loud and clear," he replied.

He'd explained to Tim on the phone the night before to use channel nine to contact the boat but to have the handheld radio ready on channel sixty-eight, so *nobody* could hear them.

He knew from experience that the little VHF walkie-talkies only had a range of about half a mile.

"The house was dark about two hours ago," Ringo said into the radio's microphone. "But we saw four men and a girl leave in the crab boat. *That* girl wasn't the blonde, so she should be all alone with the rug rat."

"Yeah, you told me about the kid," Tim said. "What exactly do you want me to do with it?"

"I don't care," Ringo replied. "From what I heard, he's too little to talk, but toss him in the water if you think you need to."

Chapter
Thirty-Two

━━━━◆━━━━◆━━━━◆━━━━◆━━━━

J esse was up with the first light of dawn. He hadn't needed an alarm clock in several years and was able to awaken at whatever time he wanted. Or at least within a few minutes.

He dressed quietly, so as not to disturb Rusty, then headed to the kitchen to make a phone call. As he crossed the living room, he pulled the scrap of paper from his pocket and read it. In the kitchen, he lifted the receiver from the wall-mounted phone and jammed it between his jaw and shoulder as he read the number Natalie had given him and dialed the phone.

She answered before the first ring ended. "Jesse?"

"Yeah. How'd you know?"

"Nobody else would be calling at sunrise," she whispered.

"Russ said yeah. But my grandfather's coming too. And I'm dropping Henry off at the airport on the way."

"Good, I'll have someone to talk to while y'all are underwater."

Just then, Pap and Henry entered the living room from the hallway.

"See," Henry whispered. "I told ya he wouldn't leave that young lady hangin'."

"I'll pick you up in thirty minutes," Jesse said.

"I can drive my own—"

"Your uncle's going to put a new battery in it," Jesse said. "I gotta go. So I'll see you in half an hour, alright?

"Okay," she whispered softly. "Bye."

"Bye," he said back, then hung up the phone. He turned to the two old men. "I told her I'd pick her up in thirty minutes."

"Doable," Henry said, picking up his flight bag. "I'm all set."

Pap shook Henry's hand. "I'm going to give Russ a hand here, so I'll say so long now and see you Tuesday morning. I have a late morning flight out of Jacksonville that'll arrive in Fort Myers an hour ahead of Norma's."

"I'll be wheels down as the sun comes up," Henry replied, then turned to Jesse. "Are *you* ready?"

Jesse held up the keys dangling on his finger. "Let's go."

Ten minutes later, they pulled into the tiny airport and Jesse just drove straight out to where Henry's Beaver sat, tied down.

"What's a plane like that cost?" Jesse asked, as they both climbed out of the Jeep.

"Depends on how ya want it set up," he replied, as he reached in back and grabbed his flight bag. "Everything stock with standard landing gear? You could probably find one for about ten grand."

"How else would you set it up?" Jesse asked, striding toward the plane with Henry.

"Like this," the old flyer replied, kicking the big balloon tire. He opened the door and put his bag on the co-pilot's seat, then started walking around the plane, checking things. "A plane that don't need a lot of room is called a 'bush plane,'" he explained. "And the Beaver's one of the best bush planes there is." He pulled the wheel chocks out on that side, then added, "I can put her down on just about any terrain that's clear of trees and boulders for two hundred feet. She's got big wings that provide a lot of lift."

"Two hundred feet?" Jesse repeated. "That opens up a lot of places."

"In winter, I can put skis on her," he said, moving the control surfaces at the back of the plane. "That opens up a lot more places. I can fish remote spots on the Great Lakes, or land her on a glacier way up in Alaska."

"What about pontoons for landing in the water?"

Henry nodded as he pulled the second pair of chocks away from the other tire. "They're called floats; boats have pontoons. There's lots of floatin' Beavers around."

"Thanks for bringing Pap out here," Jesse said. "It's weird. He seems totally different away from home like this."

"Seems the *same* to me," Henry said. "Maybe he sees *you* different, now that you're a grown man."

Could that be it? Jesse thought as Henry pulled the door closed and waved. *Does Pap see me as a peer?*

"Gimme a hand walkin' the prop?" Henry asked. "Tall as you are, it'll be easy."

"Walking the prop?" Jesse asked, as they moved to the front of the plane.

"See these cylinders on the bottom of the engine?" Henry asked, pointing. "Oil can seep past the rings and get into the head, causing hydro-lock."

Jesse nodded in understanding. "Liquids aren't compressible."

Henry raised an eyebrow. "Exactly. Quickest way to blow a motor is for it to start with oil in one of the combustion chambers."

"What do you want me to do?"

"Reach up there and pull the prop down," he said, climbing into the pilot's seat, and propping the door open with his foot. "Cycling the engine by hand for three revolutions allows any oil to drain out the exhaust valves."

With the oversized balloon tires, the prop's hub was just above Jesse's head, but he had no trouble reaching the blade.

"It won't start when I do this, will it?"

"Magneto's off," Henry replied.

Jesse pulled down on the blade, moving the engine through compression cycles of at least one cylinder, then continued pushing until he'd made half a turn. Then he repeated the process of "walking the prop" five more times for three full revolutions.

"I could do that with the electric starter," Henry said. "But it produces a whole lot more torque, and if one of the cylinders was hydro-locked, it could damage the engine."

"What do you do if you're alone?" Jesse asked. "That prop's about as high as I can reach."

"Bump the starter a little at a time through each cylinder's compression stroke, for three revolutions. But that puts a lot of stress on the starter's contact points."

He reached down and extended his hand. "It's good to finally meet you. Whenever me and Frank got together over the last eighteen years, you've been all he's talked about."

Jesse shook his hand. "It's been a pleasure."

Henry closed the door, and after a couple of minutes, opened a little side window and yelled, "Clear prop!"

Jesse took a few steps back as the starter motor engaged. The engine caught quickly, stuttering as it belched blue-gray smoke for a few seconds, then revved higher, firing smoothly.

Jesse watched the plane waddle on its oversized tires as it rolled off

the concrete onto the asphalt taxiway, then climbed into the Jeep and sat watching as the plane moved to the far end of the runway. There, Henry turned it into the wind and stopped for a moment.

The plane started moving, quickly gathering speed, and the roaring sound of the engine finally reached Jesse's ears. The tail came up, and in less distance than a football field, the plane lifted into the air, climbed a little, then banked low and slow right over Jesse's head.

He spun around and watched Henry's plane disappear over the dune vegetation, then rise up as he turned south, soaring out past the beach, just a hundred feet above the water.

"That's cool," Jesse whispered, as he turned the key in the Jeep's ignition.

Five minutes later, when he pulled up in front of Natalie's house, she was already coming out the door. As she climbed in, Jesse shifted to reverse and started backing out. "You were waiting?"

"I didn't want to hear Andy go on about the battery," she said. "I have money for one and don't need him buying one for me. I just figured if I could keep getting jump starts for a while longer…"

"It'll what?" he asked. "Grow stronger?" He glanced over at her for a moment. "Sorry. I can be too critical sometimes."

"The island's thirteen miles long," she retorted, as the Jeep started down the street. "But only ten square miles. I know everyone who has a car and can get a ride or a jump any time I see someone. And if I don't, well, you can literally walk anywhere."

"You don't like it here?" Jesse asked. "It seems pretty nice to me."

"My aunt is my only close relative," she replied. "She's my mom's only sibling, so I don't have any first cousins either. But just about everyone is related one way or another here. I thought about joining the military, but I have to finish school first."

"Solid idea," he replied. "You graduate in a couple more months, right?"

"Yeah… all six of us."

"Six?" he asked, slowing at a stop sign. "Your whole graduating class is six people?"

"The whole *school's* only a hundred kids," she said. "Kindergarten through twelfth grade."

"You guys must be pretty close," Jesse guessed.

"I'll graduate with Lauri, a second cousin," she began, ticking off a finger, "two third cousins, Janice and Steve, and two guys I've known since I was little but am probably not related to."

"Where would you go?" Jesse asked. "If you could go anywhere?"

"New York City," she replied without a second's hesitation. "As many people around me as possible."

"Fort Myers isn't *that* big," he said. "But it's a good-sized city, and growing. I think I'd like something in between here and there."

"That's why I was thinking of joining up," she said. "I'd always be around others, meeting new people, and seeing something besides sand and water."

"Have you ever been to the Keys?" he asked.

"I've only been off the island a few times," she replied. "One time, all the way to Raleigh."

"My friend Rusty is from there," Jesse said. "His is a small town too, but I think his class was about thirty or so. Mine was over two hundred."

"I'd take either of those," she said, as Jesse turned into Russ's driveway. "You must have a lot of friends back home."

"Not a lot," Jesse said, steering the Jeep back to its spot and shutting off the engine. "Just one who I'd call a really close friend—Billy Rainwater."

"Rainwater?"

"He's Calusa Indian," Jesse said, climbing out. "His dad's the chieftain."

Natalie jumped out and met him in front of the Jeep. "For real? Like the chief of the tribe?"

"Not exactly," he replied. "The Calusa people are led by a group of elders, and Leaping Panther—that's his Calusa name —he's the head of the elder council, since he's the only one who's pure Calusa. He became sort of an uncle to me, I guess, after my folks died. He and my dad were real close too."

When they turned the corner of the house, Jesse could see the others out on the dock and waved to them.

"So, you're like the boy in *The Light in the Forest*?"

He looked down at her and smiled. "True-son? I don't think

I'd go *that* far. He lived with the Indians most of his life. I learned a lot from Leaping Panther, but my grandparents raised me."

She looked down at the ground as they walked. "Will you ever come back here after this week, Jesse McDermitt?"

Chapter
Thirty-Three

$\leftarrow\!\!\!\!\bullet\!\!-\!\!\bullet\!\!-\!\!\bullet\!\!-\!\!\bullet\!\!\!\!\rightarrow$

O nce Russ cleared the inlet, he turned north-northeast, angling slowly away from the coast and toward the massive sandbars off Cape Hatteras—the Graveyard of the Atlantic.

As Jesse and Rusty began assembling their gear, Pap watched with interest. "How deep will you be diving?" he asked.

"A little over eighty feet," Jesse replied. "The tide's lower today, though."

"You can't stay very long at that depth," he said, a hint of worry in his tone.

"Can't stay down long in this cold water, either," Rusty said. "This is the coldest water I ever been in."

Natalie stood at the wheelhouse door, arms crossed and rubbing them with her hands. "Not much different than the air today."

Jesse finished assembling his rig, checked the air pressure and flow, then strapped the tank in place as Natalie went into the wheelhouse. He followed her and stood by the door.

"Take over," Russ said to Natalie, as he stepped away from the wheel. "Keep the compass on twenty-five degrees while I get the sat-nav system up and running. Have you ever used one of these?"

She glanced over at it as Russ bent to enter the latitude and longitude of the wreck.

"You tell it where you want to go?" Natalie replied. "And it points the way?"

"Close enough," he said, pointing at the heading displayed on the little screen. "Just keep the compass on whatever this tells you, and we'll be there in a few hours."

She leaned over to read the screen. "Got it."

Russ stepped out of the small wheelhouse and Jesse entered, moving up beside her.

"You look like a natural," he said. "You've done a lot of boating?"

She looked over at him and smiled, the early morning sun shining on her cheek. "Ten-square-mile island, remember? Kids around here learn to drive a boat years before a car. I drove Dad's boat before I learned to ride a bike."

"My grandfather builds boats," Jesse told her, putting a hand on the seat's armrest to steady himself in the rolling boat. "He and I built four from the time I was eight years old, up until two years ago. A fifth one is about half finished."

"What kind of boats?" she asked. "Little ones?"

"Three sailboats," Jesse replied, swaying easily with the boat's movement. "The biggest was thirty-four feet. Plus a twenty-foot fishing boat, and the one we're building now is a thirty-foot cruiser with an inboard diesel."

She looked over at him again just as the boat lurched to the left, pushed by a wave hitting the side of the hull. When she reached out her free hand for the armrest, she grabbed Jesse's hand resting there.

"Oops," she said, looking forward again, but not letting go.

"Yeah, oops," he said, and they both laughed.

"We already kissed," she said softly. "So holding hands is kind of a step back."

Pap and Russ were leaning on the gunwale just forward of the wheelhouse, talking, and Pap glanced through the window at them together at the helm. A corner of his mouth ticked up and he gave Jesse an almost imperceptible nod.

Jesse had dated a few girls in high school, and Pap had never given any sort of indication of approving of any of them, even if Jesse'd come right out and asked his opinion. Nor had he ever said anything disapproving.

"It's not for me to decide," was always his standard answer.

Mam had always nodded, adding, "In matters of the heart, you and you alone must decide."

Was Pap's nod meant for Natalie? She was pretty, but not a dainty little wallflower. She seemed perfectly at home driving the boat, glancing down at the compass now and then, but made course corrections based more on wave activity, turning into the low rollers as they approached.

Jesse found himself wondering what Mam would think of her.

The warning from Russ about the women on Court Street ran head on into his mind, right into the thought of Pap or Mam approving.

There were quite a few divorcées around the base, many

from Japan and Vietnam, all looking for a new husband; one who was on his way up in rank.

Jesse was already a lance corporal, and he hadn't been in the Corps a whole year yet. He hoped to make sergeant by the end of his first enlistment, or immediately after re-enlisting. If he could reach gunnery sergeant in less than twelve years, he'd likely retire at the highest enlisted rank, sergeant major.

He wondered for a moment what Natalie might be willing to do to leave Ocracoke. She'd mentioned joining the military so she could see the world and meet more people.

Follow your last order first.

It was something both Pap and Russ had told him. Applying that to everyday events outside the Marine Corps, he decided it meant to live more in the moment and not worry about the what ifs. Jesse couldn't help but smile as he rolled with the boat.

Do what feels right.

"You asked earlier if I planned to come back here," he said. "It's not far from the base; the ferry ride's the longest part of the drive."

"And if you take care of Mr. Livingston's Jeep," she began, then squeezed his hand. "You could drive up for a weekend, maybe?"

"Highly possible," he replied. "But I really should get another car."

"You had one before?"

"Some guy torched it," he replied. "It was a boot camp graduation gift from Pap."

"What an asshole," she said, turning the boat into a wave. "Why'd he do that?"

"Because I ratted him out for murder," Jesse replied, looking off toward shore.

He couldn't see anything but water and figured they were probably four or five miles offshore and a good eight miles from the inlet.

"Murder?" she asked, clearly a little shocked at his explanation.

Jesse shrugged. "A woman was killed while Rusty and I were in the Keys, and I'd seen her riding on the back of the guy's motorcycle less than an hour before."

There was a beep from the dashboard.

"What's that?" Natalie asked, pointing at the radar screen.

Jesse bent closer. There was a white blob behind them. He looked back but didn't see anything.

"I don't know," he replied, then pushed the side window open further. "Hey, Russ. What's the radar range set at?"

"Max distance," he replied. "About twenty-four miles. Something on the screen?"

Jesse watched the blob on the circular display for a moment. He had no idea how to operate it, or even interpret what it meant, but he'd seen radar in movies and TV shows before, and knew the blob represented a boat or ship.

If the distance between the center, where they were, and the blob at the bottom of the screen was twenty or so miles, then whatever it was, it was moving pretty fast, getting closer with every sweep of the line spinning around the screen.

Russ entered the wheelhouse with them and looked at the radar screen. After just a moment, it was obvious that whatever it was, it was heading toward the inlet and moving pretty fast.

"Another drug boat," Russ muttered, as Rusty stepped inside.

"Hey, did your wife ever call that guy selling the trawler?"

"I forgot to ask her," he replied, then reached for the radio microphone. "Howard House, Howard House, this is *Dauntless* calling on six-eight."

"You have a radio at the house?" Rusty asked.

Natalie turned and nodded. "Nearly every house on the island has a marine-band radio."

Russ repeated the call.

"We're at least seven or eight miles away," Jesse said. "Probably out of range."

"You didn't see the antenna sticking up above the big live oak tree beside the house?" Russ asked. "It's over a hundred feet high, and the one on the roof of the boat here is twenty feet above the water."

Jesse knew radio waves couldn't bend with the curve of the earth, and he also knew the calculation for determining the distance to the horizon, the farthest a regular VHF radio could reach.

"That should give you a range of more than thirteen miles, then," Jesse advised. "If she has it on."

"It stays on," Russ said. "And Suze never gets far from it if I'm out on the water."

He made the call a third time and Suzanne's voice came over the speaker, broken up with static.

"*Daunt*—ssss, *Dauntless*, this—ssss Howard ssss. I'm out in the shop."

"Do me a favor, Suze," Russ said into the mic, speaking

slowly. "Call Hal and ask him who the guy is that's interested in his boat."

"Stand by, *Daunt*—*ssss*. I'll have to ssss up to the house."

"She's using the radio in the shop," Russ said. "It can pick us up, better than we can hear her."

A few minutes ticked by, then Suzanne called back.

"This is *Dauntless*," Russ said. "Go ahead."

"Hal said he heard what happened last night," Suzanne said, her voice much clearer. "He apologized for that, and said the man's name is Richard Thomas, but he prefers to be called Ringo. He paid cash and they closed the deal early this morning."

"That's weird," Russ said, without keying the mic. "It's Sunday and the banks are closed."

He glanced down at the radar screen again, pressed the mic button, and said, "We're seeing another one of those drug boats heading toward the inlet."

The blob on the radar screen became two blobs, both just outside the mouth of the inlet.

"That's another boat headin' out," Rusty said, as the first one disappeared through the inlet, and was lost in the back scatter of the island. "Any guess as to who it could be? Maybe they can turn back and watch your house for a minute."

"No idea," Russ replied, as the outward-bound blob started turning toward the south. He keyed the mic again. "Suzanne! Do you read me?"

Ssss…

There was silence for a moment, then Suzanne's voice came over the speaker again. "I see ssss. It's the same blue ssss as the other day."

"She's back on the shop radio," Russ said, puzzled. "What the hell's she doing out there?"

"Two drug runs?" Rusty asked. "That's risky after being spotted by the law last night– I don't care how fast their boat is."

"*Daunt—ssss, Dauntless*," Suzanne said, urgency in her voice. "The ssss boat is coming toward our ssss."

The radio hissed for several seconds, and all Jesse could make out was "at our dock."

"Load up, Suze!" Russ yelled into the mic. "Suze, load up and bug out now!

Chapter Thirty-Four

◆———◆———◆———◆———◆

V*engeance,* Jesse thought, feeling acid burn in his gut.

He hoped it wasn't. He hoped that it was just a random boat they were seeing on the radar. But what if they'd found out where Russ lived and had waited for them to leave in order to go after his wife in retribution for what happened at the bar?

Was Pap right? Was letting others push you around acceptable under certain circumstances?

Jesse was hyperaware and cognizant of it. Information bombarded his mind from senses that were gathering and sending at high speed, making it seem as if everything around him was slowing down while his mind urged it to go faster.

"I have the wheel," Russ said, crowding Natalie aside and turning the boat directly into an oncoming swell. The bow came down with a heavy thud and slap of water.

Between waves, he turned again, putting the rollers behind them and slightly to the left. He pushed the throttle all the way forward as he steered a reciprocal course home.

Pap leaned in through the open door. "What's wrong?"

A wave lifted the stern, tilting the boat forward and to the right, increasing its speed a little.

"Suzanne!" Russ nearly shouted into the mic. "What's going on?"

There was silence, and Jesse turned toward Pap. "She said that blue racing boat was back and headed toward their dock."

"Howard House! Howard House!" Russ called, trying to jam the throttle even more.

Jesse looked down at the little speedometer on the dash. It was almost like a car's and read miles per hour instead of knots. They were going all of twelve miles per hour, or ten and a half knots. It was going to take them at least forty minutes to get back.

They rode mostly in silence, with Russ calling on one channel for Suzanne, then switching to others hailing the Coast Guard, the sheriff's boat, or anyone at all who might be able to help. They were just too far from shore and the radio not powerful enough.

Twenty minutes later, *Dauntless* had covered half the distance back to the inlet as the second radar return continued south, though it looked to Jesse as if they'd gained on it a little.

A growing sense of dread crept over Jesse as he looked around at the hard faces of his friends and grandfather, and the frightened look Natalie gave him.

He didn't sense that she was feeling fear for herself, but rather for the situation that might be going on at Russ's house. He put an arm around her, and she put her head on his shoulder but kept her eyes on the radar screen.

They should have canceled the day's dive, Jesse thought. They should have at least considered the idea that those guys might come back looking for trouble. Wasn't that what criminals did?

Suddenly, another radar return appeared, coming out of the inlet, which was almost within sight.

Jesse stepped outside and climbed up on the gunwale, holding onto the handrail as he looked ahead. He lifted his head as high as possible, straining his eyes to see. The stern came up as another wave overtook them and then lifted the whole boat higher.

"Dead ahead!" Jesse shouted over the wind and waves. "It's the blue racing boat!"

"It's turnin' south too," Rusty called up to him from the wheelhouse door. "Looks like it's followin' that other boat."

Jesse lost sight of the boat as soon as *Dauntless* rode down the shoulder of the wave and into the trough. He looked behind them, willing the next wave to move faster. Finally, the stern started coming up, and he looked forward again.

"Still see it?" Rusty yelled.

Jesse scanned the water ahead. The time between waves had only been about fifteen seconds, but he knew that the blue boat could cover a lot of water in that time, up to a quarter mile.

"Nothing," Jesse said, climbing down again. "Already out of sight."

"Try Aunt Sophie on channel seventeen," Natalie suggested. "We should be close enough for Andy's little radio and he might still be at home."

Russ switched the radio frequency and handed Natalie the mic.

She pressed the button on the side. "Aunt Sophie, Aunt Sophie, this is Natalie aboard *Dauntless*. Do you read me?"

A woman replied after just a couple of seconds. "Natalie? Is something wrong?"

Russ took the mic from her and keyed it. "No time to explain, Sophie. This is Russ Livingston. Is Andy at home? I think something might be going on at my house."

There was a pause, then, just as Russ started to bring the mic back up to his mouth, Deputy Barret's voice came over the speaker. "Russ, this is Andy. What's going on?"

"Do you know if Hal's boat is at the marina?" he asked, an edge to his voice.

"Stand by." A moment later, Andy replied. "Negative. The trawler's gone. What's going on, Russ?"

"I need you to go to my house," Russ said. "Suzanne saw that blue drug runner again, about fifteen minutes ago, and it was headed toward our dock. Now she's not answering."

There was another moment of silence, then Natalie's aunt came back on the air. "He just bolted out the door," she said. "He'll be on this channel in just a few seconds."

Jesse looked at the radar screen. If it was twenty-four miles from the center to the outer edge of the circle on the screen, it looked like they'd gained almost a mile on the slower boat, which was now very close to the blue boat, probably four miles ahead.

"They stopped!" Russ exclaimed, as the two blobs merged into just a single radar return. "And they're real close together."

"Russ," a voice called from the speaker, quite clear. "It's Andy. I'm headed over to your house now. Is there anything I don't know about but probably should?"

Russ paused for only a second, then keyed the mic. "We had a bit of an altercation last night at Howard's Pub with the men on that blue boat, and one of them is the guy who bought Hal's big trawler. I think both boats are about three miles south of the inlet, stationary, but they *were* headed south."

"I'll get dispatch to send Clyde out," Andy replied. "He's probably the closest. How far offshore are the two boats?"

Jesse knew instantly why he'd asked that question. Andy Barret was local law enforcement and would have no jurisdiction beyond three miles from shore.

Russ looked at the radar screen, then keyed the mic. "Right now, they're about four miles south of the inlet and four miles offshore."

"I'll alert Coast Guard Sector North Carolina in Wilmington, too," Andy said. "I'll be at your house in less than five minutes, though. I'm sure everything's okay."

The seconds felt like minutes, and the minutes like an eternity as all five of them crowded into the wheelhouse, with Jesse and Pap at the door.

"There's the inlet buoys," Natalie said, pointing off to the right and slightly forward. "We're way outside the markers."

Russ glanced at the radar, then turned a little more southerly, away from the inlet.

"You're going after the two boats?" Pap asked him.

"Just in case," Russ replied, his knuckles white on the wheel.

Another couple of minutes ticked by, then the radio crackled. "Russ, this is Andy. Do you copy?"

"I got you, Andy," he replied, his voice breaking slightly as he pushed on the throttle for about the tenth time. "Are my wife and son okay?"

The pause was only a couple of seconds but seemed like forever.

"The boy's here, Russ," Andy said. "He's okay. But there's no sign of Suzanne."

Chapter Thirty-Five

◆━━━━◆━━━◆━━━◆━━━━◆

Wﾐﾐﾐith the knowledge that his son was safe, the Coast
Guard down in Wilmington alerted about the possible
abduction, and the other deputy just about to leave the marina,
Russ had no choice but to turn straight toward the two boats,
still represented by a single radar return.

"If nothing else," he told the others, "we'll at least be able to
track them on radar until help arrives."

If both boats maintained the speed of the slower trawler.

There was no solid evidence that Suzanne had been taken
against her will, nor that she was on the blue boat, but everything seemed to be pointing in that direction, just as sure as
she'd pointed her gun at the leader, Richard "Ringo" Thomas.

If these people were drug runners, Jesse thought, *then they'd be
dangerous.*

He had to assume they weren't stupid. The dumb ones
would mostly be in prison. That would explain why they'd
backed down when confronted at the bar.

To keep a low profile? he thought. People who smuggled drugs wouldn't want to draw any kind of attention.

Were they then seeking retribution now that the job was done?

Jesse pushed past Pap, with those and many other questions in his mind. He climbed up on the gunwale to his lookout position.

They were past the inlet and only three or four miles away from the two boats. He figured he should be able to see them at that range, and wanted to know for certain who and what the other boat was.

A wave raised the stern, and as it lifted the boat, Jesse saw the trawler with the racing boat alongside it. They seemed to be stopped and either tied off or drifting so close together they'd bump.

"I see the boats!" he called down to the others.

"Here," Pap said, handing up a pair of binoculars. "I already focused them on infinity."

Jesse took the binos in his right hand and held them up to his eyes while hanging on with his left. After scanning the water for a moment, he saw the two boats clearly.

And Suzanne Livingston.

"They've got her on the trawler!" he shouted. "The big guy has her on the swim platform!"

"Oh my God!" Natalie cried out.

"Can you see what they're doing?" Russ yelled.

"The blue boat's casting off," Jesse called down, keeping his voice as calm as possible. "Only one guy in the blue boat, and the big man is pushing it away."

Jesse watched as the guy they called Moose took Suzanne by

the arm and forced her up the rear steps of the trawler to the cockpit.

Suzanne stumbled on the last step and Jesse's blood began to boil as he jerked her up roughly. There were two other men there. One of them was the new owner, Richard Thomas.

The giant turned and pointed a finger straight at the approaching *Dauntless*, just as he'd done the other night as their boat had raced through the inlet.

"They spotted us, Russ!" Jesse yelled down to the wheelhouse. "The big man, along with the guy we think is Richard Thomas, just took Suzanne into the trawler's cabin."

"What do you think they're going to do?" Natalie asked, her voice quaking in fear.

Pap put a comforting arm around the girl. "We'll get her back. Don't you worry."

The racing boat roared away from the trawler, leaping on top of the water, then turning, then racing straight toward *Dauntless*, pounding over the wavetops at a mile a minute.

"We're gonna have comp'ny pretty quick!" Rusty shouted, now standing on the opposite gunwale.

Jesse didn't know a lot about the smuggling world, but he had to assume these guys had guns. With the blue boat headed straight at them, he felt uncomfortable and exposed.

The water roiled up at the stern of the larger boat.

"The trawler's moving now!" Jesse shouted. "Any idea how big it is, Russ?"

"Fifty-three feet," Natalie called back. "Why?"

"Hull speed's around nine knots, then!" Rusty answered. "Prolly less! We can outrun the trawler!"

"Right!" Jesse exclaimed, as the blue boat got closer, then

suddenly started to slow down. "But we have to contend with that guy first."

As he watched, no longer needing the binos, the racing boat slowed to a stop, no more than half a mile ahead of them.

Dauntless continued on, the diesel winding as high as it would go, pushing the heavy boat through the water at full speed.

"He's stopped!" Rusty yelled. "What the hell's he think he's gonna do? Block us with a plastic toy or somethin'?"

Jesse raised the binos again, just in time to see the man in the blue boat stand up with an oar or something. It was the guy Pap almost choked out, Tim. At first, Jesse thought the boat might've broken down.

Until the guy braced the oar over the windshield.

"Incoming fire!" Jesse shouted as he saw the puff of smoke from the barrel of the rifle.

Neither he nor Rusty took cover, and the sound of the bullet passing far over their heads cracked the air like a bolt of lightning.

Natalie screamed.

Russ slowed the boat and a moment later appeared in the cockpit with his own rifle, quickly mounting the gunwale.

"Hold me in place," he said, as he raised an older Remington rifle above the roof.

Jesse moved his right hand around Russ and grabbed the rail, pinning him to the roof's edge with his body, then sliding the binos over to Rusty.

Russ racked the bolt back, then slammed it forward, chambering a round. With his head and shoulders above the roof, he sighted in on the boat, just as a second bullet screamed past *Dauntless* like an angry hornet, wide to the left but closer.

At that distance, and from a rocking boat, the average shooter would never be able to aim with any degree of accuracy, even at something as big as their boat, but there was always the chance of a lucky shot.

However, Russ Livingston wasn't an average shooter.

He fired.

"A hit!" Rusty shouted, watching through the binos. "The left side of the windshield anyway! He's hightailin' it."

"Give me the rifle, Russ," Jesse said, his tone firm and even. "We can't let that boat get back to the trawler."

"No, Jesse," Pap said from below. "You can't—"

Russ racked the bolt and fired again.

"Way high!" Rusty shouted.

"Give me the gun, Russ. We can't outrun *that* boat."

Reluctantly, Russ exchanged positions with Jesse, holding him in place so he could try to disable the racing boat.

Dauntless rocked in the light chop, the engine idling in neutral as all of Jesse's senses heightened. He could hear the wave approaching the stern and felt the subtle movement of the boat between waves. *Dauntless* dipped forward and rose, surfing down the wave a little before the roller passed under her and she settled back down in the trough.

Jesse aimed the rifle. It felt very familiar in his hands, yet a little different than his own 700, which he'd probably fired several thousand rounds with.

"Zeroed at three hundred yards," Russ whispered in his ear. "Range approximately five hundred. Wind's from the left. Value three. Rollers are at eleven-second intervals."

Jesse didn't have time to adjust the rifle's windage or elevation from the information Russ gave him and which he instinctively knew. He used "Kentucky windage" to aim at a point just above and slightly left of his target—the wide stern of the escaping boat. A bullet anywhere in the engine compartment would likely disable it.

The front and rear sights melded together as Jesse controlled his breathing. His cheek became one with the rifle's stock, and his lower body was fixed to the boat by Russ's arm around his waist.

The racing boat was picking up speed, nearly five hundred yards ahead of them.

It wasn't the distance that concerned Jesse. He'd hit dead center with every shot at the five-hundred-yard line both in boot camp and at infantry school. Recently, he'd hit four out of five at eight hundred yards.

But that'd been in a prone firing position.

Allowing only his upper body to move, swaying to counter the movement of the boat, Jesse kept the open sights glued to an imaginary spot just above the broken left corner of the wind-shield as he slowly exhaled.

His finger deliberately took the slack out of the trigger, knowing that if he hit the gas tank or the man at the wheel, the guy was going to be dead.

He could feel Pap's stare.

The rifle boomed and bucked in his hands, the recoil pushing Jesse's shoulder back, but he knew the shot was true.

A second later, flames started erupting from the back of the blue boat as it continued to race toward the trawler. The speed of the boat created a wind that fanned the flames, and they grew in intensity.

"Looks like you hit one of the engines!" Rusty shouted. "He's slowin' down."

Russ jumped down and went back into the wheelhouse. A second later, *Dauntless* was underway again, the diesel engine screaming in protest.

Suddenly, the racing boat veered to the left, just as a massive explosion ripped it in half, sending debris in all directions.

An orange and black fireball rolled upward against the clear blue sky.

Chapter
Thirty-Six

$\longleftarrow\!\!\!\blacklozenge\!\!\!-\!\!\!\blacklozenge\!\!\!-\!\!\!\blacklozenge\!\!\!\longrightarrow$

The trawler was at least two miles ahead and running flat out toward the south as *Dauntless* passed the debris field, some larger pieces still aflame. Russ didn't even give it a look as they got closer to the men who'd taken his wife. With a slight speed advantage, they'd been closing the distance at a rate of about two miles an hour.

They needed help, and quick, but were now out of radio range with anyone on Ocracoke. *Dauntless* could catch the much larger boat, but it would be a slow and anxious process. And then what? Those guys were bound to have more guns, and all they had on *Dauntless* was Russ's rifle and a flare gun.

The only thing Thomas had to do was wait for *Dauntless* to get close enough, then open fire. The bigger boat was a lot more stable a shooting platform when both boats were under way.

"What do we do now?" Rusty asked. "Where the hell's the cops?"

Russ checked the radar. "The inlet's six miles behind us and still no sign of Clyde in Andy's boat. It isn't much faster than we are."

"How fast?" Jesse asked.

Russ looked over at him. "Top speed's twenty miles an hour."

"He'll still be at least fifteen minutes behind us when we catch up to the trawler."

Russ stared at him for a moment. "I'll just assume that's correct, so we'll have to slow them down somehow until Clyde catches up."

Pap shook his head. "We know there are at least three people on that boat, not counting your wife. We have to assume they're all armed. We'll be outgunned."

"But not outmanned," Rusty said, then turned to Jesse. "Think you can get prone up there on the roof?"

Jesse looked at him a moment, then at Russ, before stepping outside and up to the gunwale again.

The radar's array was low profile and mounted toward the front of the roof, so it was above the front roof pillars of the wheelhouse. The top was nearly two feet above the roof, but it had a good twelve inches below it. Prone, his muzzle would only be eight.

Jesse jumped back down, with Rusty's thought already planting the seed for the outline of a plan.

"Yeah," he replied to Russ. "The seas aren't much except the rollers, and the range will be minimal. I have the same rifle back home and have used it a lot."

"What are you talking about?" Natalie asked.

He grinned down at her. "It's *my* turn to ride shotgun."

Rusty nudged Russ. "Pap drives, Jesse covers us from the

roof, and me and you stand up on the bow and jump aboard when Pap rams the stern. Whatta ya think?"

"Rams the…" Pap began, then looked again at the big trawler more than a mile in the distance. "It might work. It'll be a soft hit at worst and that big swim platform will absorb must of it. But I'm going with you two. Natalie can drive the boat."

"You can't," Jesse protested. "You're too—"

"Too what, Jesse?" Pap said, his face hardened with concern. "Too old? I think that man you blew to smithereens might argue that point after I tossed him around last night."

"Sorry, sir."

They all looked at Natalie, and Russ was the first to speak. "You think you can do it?"

She looked around at the four of them. "You're all trained soldiers," she said nervously. "I'm just—"

"Just one of the best crab boat pilots on Pamlico Sound," Russ interrupted. "At least that's what your dad once told me." Then he winked. "And we're Marines, not soldiers."

She bit her lower lip and nodded. "I can do it. But what if one of you falls in? What if they start shooting?"

"I know I can keep them pinned down," Jesse said. "How much ammo do you have?"

Russ opened an overhead compartment and felt around inside.

"Six rounds left in that mag with one in the pipe," he said, pulling a second magazine out. "And a fresh ten here."

Jesse took the magazine, removed the one in the rifle, and replaced it with the full one. With the round still in the chamber and a fresh mag, he wouldn't have to reload for eleven shots.

He dropped the lighter magazine into his left pocket. "Are you sure you don't want to wait for Clyde or the Coast Guard?"

"I'm not asking any of you to do this," Russ said, then turned to Pap, the only other married person. "My wife's on that boat."

Pap nodded and turned to face Jesse and Rusty. "Clyde won't reach that boat for fifteen minutes after we do. Fifteen minutes could be a long time for Miss Suzanne." He paused and then went on in a more serious tone. "Sometimes, a man is *forced* to take the law into his own hands."

Chapter Thirty-Seven

———◆———◆———◆———◆———

W hen they were still half a mile behind the trawler, and more than four miles off the coast, Natalie pointed at the radar screen.

"That's got to be Clyde," she said. "And maybe Andy too. He'd almost have to go right by your house coming out of Silver Lake."

"He's almost eight miles back," Rusty said. "If I'm guessin' right."

"You are," Russ replied, taking the mic and holding it close to his mouth. "Hyde County Sheriff's boat, Hyde County Sheriff's boat, this is Russ Livingston aboard *Dauntless*. Do you copy?"

There was nothing but static.

"Too far away," Natalie said. "They probably can't hear us yet."

"He'll catch the trawler in less than an hour," Jesse said. "We'll catch it in less than that—twenty minutes—well before

Clyde will even have visual. And they'll be in shooting range in less than ten."

"We're on our own to stop them, gentlemen," Pap said. "May I suggest that you two go ahead of me when we board?"

Rusty looked up at him. "I don't think you'd slow us—"

"Oh, I didn't mean that," Pap said. "I'm old but I'm not dead. I was thinking only of mass. You two go left and right, and I'll go up the middle."

Russ maneuvered *Dauntless* just inside the wake of the much larger boat, then motioned Natalie closer.

"Stay out of the middle," he cautioned, pointing to the bubbling white water extending behind the trawler. "That bubbly water will cause us to lose buoyancy and slow down." He pointed along the left wake. "Stay close behind the wave all the way to the boat. There's a little bulge of water behind it. You want to ride that bulge until I signal you."

"Then what?" she asked, nervously taking the wheel.

"Cut the wheel hard to the right, then immediately hard to the left," Russ replied. "That'll put you right in the prop wash, and *Dauntless* will slow a lot, just as we hit their swim platform."

"There's a guy on the stern," Rusty said, pointing.

Just as everyone turned to look, the man in the trawler's cockpit brought up a rifle.

A semi-automatic with a scope.

"Time to get to work," Jesse said, unconcerned. "We're pretty close, Russ. How about turning off the radar? It'll be a distraction."

They were close enough to see that it was the local guy from Hatteras. He was only brandishing the weapon; they were still too far away for any kind of accuracy, and once they were close enough, the scope would be far less of a benefit.

Russ switched off the radar unit and the screen went blank.

"Son," Pap said, putting a hand on Jesse's shoulder. "You don't fire unless fired upon."

Jesse nodded and picked up the rifle. He started to turn, but Russ grabbed his arm.

"I appreciate what you're doing, Jesse. All of you."

"You'd do the same," Pap said, putting a hand on both his and Jesse's shoulders. "I know now that the bond in peace time is just as great."

"We'll get her back, Russ," Jesse assured him, then went out the door and stepped up onto the gunwale.

Rusty followed him and held the rifle as Jesse climbed up onto the roof on all fours, just behind the radar array.

Dauntless continued eating up the distance and was now only about four hundred yards behind. Jesse didn't have to do the math to know that a collision was going to happen in just a few minutes.

The radar array had stopped almost in line with the boat, which put it completely out of Jesse's way as he spread his legs out, hooking his ankles around the rails.

The cold wind blasted his face, and he judged that the trawler was now only three hundred yards ahead.

"Gimme the rifle!"

Rusty moved along the gunwale, hanging on with his right hand and holding the rifle and binos in his left. Once he handed off the rifle, he hooked his right arm under the grab rail along the roof's edge and brought the binos up for a closer look.

Jesse got himself situated with the rifle, flipped off the safety, and took aim.

The man on the trawler seemed surprised at the overt action he was seeing and raised his own rifle.

"Shot fired!" Rusty shouted needlessly.

At maybe the length of two football fields, seeing the puff and recoil from the man's rifle and hearing the sound of the bullet hitting the water harmlessly to starboard were nearly simultaneous inputs to Jesse's mind, and it was anticipated.

Pap had taught Jesse a good deal about fighting when it was necessary. Rule number one was to *never* throw the first punch.

The Remington boomed and the guy in the cockpit stumbled back, dropping his weapon on the deck.

Rule number two was to always hit back *harder*.

"Hit!" Rusty grunted. "But he might not be outta the fight."

Jesse quickly racked a fresh round in the chamber. His subconscious registered the fact that he'd just shot a man. But for now, it was being quiet, as his conscious mind agreed with Rusty's assessment and felt certain his shot had been slightly high and a little to the left.

The man rose, his right shoulder stained with blood. Then he brought the rifle up again, firing wildly.

Jesse exhaled and pressed the trigger.

The man was yanked backward, as if something had grabbed his head. A pink mist coated the glistening white fiberglass behind him, and the rifle fell from his lifeless hands.

"Move up to the bow!" Jesse shouted.

Rusty tossed the binos into the cockpit and moved forward as Pap followed him, and Russ went up the starboard side.

There were no rails around the foredeck, just the low

gunwales of a working boat and the anchor windlass. Russ and Rusty crouched on either side of the ground tackle, their outboard feet up on the forward part of the gunwale, ready to leap.

Pap crouched behind them, a hand on each man's waist.

Jesse thought again how Pap shouldn't be there. He *was* too old. If anything happened, Jesse'd never forgive himself.

The sliding door to the cockpit opened and the old man from the marina came out, scampering toward the dead man.

Jesse's sights were locked on his chest, the slack already out of the trigger. "Don't do it, old timer," he mumbled, his cheek welded to the stock.

Charlie Noble rose with the rifle in his hands, holding it across his body as he looked back at the quickly approaching *Dauntless*, and saw Jesse aiming at his chest from the roof.

Suddenly, he thrust both hands forward, throwing the weapon over the rail and into the water.

Chapter
Thirty-Eight

$\blacklozenge$ ━━━ $\blacklozenge$ ━━━ $\blacklozenge$ ━━━ $\blacklozenge$

R uss raised his left hand, holding tightly to the top of the windlass with the other. Jesse waited for the signal, tensing his body, hoping the rifle that Charlie Noble had dropped was the only one aboard.

Jesse could sense a change in the way *Dauntless* was moving as it got closer and closer to the stern and began to get into the prop wash below the big boat's swim platform.

The white water at the stern of a large boat like that would be full of air bubbles. Boats float on water, but not so much on air. Getting into that foamy stream at the stern would cause *Dauntless* to sink lower in the water, increasing drag and slowing her down.

Russ pumped his hand to the right and the boat turned suddenly, bogging down a little, then turning back to the left.

The bow collided with the swim platform and the light-weight structure cracked and crumbled as *Dauntless* rode up on it for a second.

Just as *Dauntless* slowed, Russ and Rusty launched themselves forward as Pap jumped between them.

All three men landed on the lower steps and the remnants of the swim platform, then quickly scrambled up to where Noble stood, hands raised, as *Dauntless* lost buoyancy and began to fall back.

Natalie steered the boat out of the prop wash and maintained speed behind the trawler, which Jesse noticed for the first time was called *Nauti Gull*.

"Stupid name!" Jesse shouted at the boat. "Get some, Marines!"

There were still at least two men on the boat—Ringo Thomas and the giant, Moose. Jesse figured they were probably in the pilothouse, and he snapped off a shot just along the port rail to get their attention.

Seven left in the mag, one in the pipe, and six more in the spare mag.

"What now?" Natalie cried out from below.

They hadn't talked about that part. The battle plan was always the first casualty and rarely survived first contact with the enemy. The fact that they'd survived the first two contacts, most likely with two enemy fatalities, made just getting them aboard a miracle.

"Hold this position behind them!" Jesse shouted down to her.

He remained in position, his rifle up and ready, body poised as another roller passed under the boat.

Several anxious minutes passed, and Jesse saw no movement on deck or through the partially open sliding door. Then *Dauntless* began to slow down, moving farther to the left.

Rusty stepped out of the pilothouse door on the port side, waving one hand over his head, then *Nauti Gull* began to slow.

Jesse climbed down from the roof and stepped into the wheelhouse.

"They just called on the radio," Natalie said. "Mr. Livingston wants me to come up to the rail opening on the side."

Jesse exhaled a long breath. He wasn't sure just how long he'd been holding it.

This was good news. It meant Russ wanted to bring Suzanne out and onto *Dauntless* without her seeing the dead man in the cockpit.

She was okay.

"Need me to do anything?" Jesse asked, stowing the rifle on the little bench seat beside the helm.

"Fenders," she replied, turning the wheel.

"Got it," Jesse said and hurried out to the cockpit.

He put two fenders over the side as the trawler slowed to a stop, and when Natalie brought *Dauntless* up beside it, he grabbed the lower part of the rail with one hand as Russ and Suzanne came out of the pilothouse.

One sleeve of her blouse was torn and several of the buttons were gone from the front.

Jesse noted the beginning of a bruise on her left cheek, and he felt his fury begin to rise again.

Pap climbed down and helped Jesse hold the two boats in position as Russ helped Suzanne into the wheelhouse.

"Where's Rusty?" he asked Pap, who was also disheveled.

"He'll be along," Pap replied, then extended his hand, which clutched the gold chain Russ had planned to give Suzanne.

When he opened his fist, it held a very large emerald, attached to the chain, and still partially encrusted.

"Thomas had this in his hand," Pap said. "Suzanne said she was cleaning it in the shop when the guy in the racing boat arrived. She said he threatened to kill the boy if she didn't show him the rest."

Suddenly, the trawler's diesels engaged, and a second later, Rusty scampered down.

The trawler's engines revved, and water bulged from behind it as the big props started turning.

Russ pushed the throttle and turned sharply away from the bigger boat, making a complete turn as the larger vessel accelerated and began to turn east.

"You're letting them go?" Jesse asked.

Rusty shook his head and pulled Jesse outside, shutting the wheelhouse door behind them.

"It's like this, bro," Rusty began. "There's two dead guys on that boat and a third got tossed overboard, plus the old man from the marina, Charlie Noble." He jerked a thumb over his shoulder toward the bow. "Not to mention another dead guy feedin' the crabs up ahead of us somewhere. You killed two and your grandpa killed the other two."

"Pap?" Jesse muttered, as he looked through the back window at his grandfather, who was putting a blanket around Suzanne and Natalie, sitting on the little bench together.

"I hope to hell I never piss him off," Rusty said, then pointed at the trawler, heading east but now just at idle speed.

The old man was lowering an inflatable dinghy off the stern. Once it was nearly in the water, he ran down to the busted swim platform and pulled the painter out, tying the bitter end to a cleat. Then he ran back up to the bridge deck and lowered the crane's cable until the painter had all the slack out.

"What's he doing?"

"Covering our tracks," Rusty said. "That boat can go a thousand miles before her tanks run dry. But the water comin' in through the bilge will reach the motors by the time its thirty or forty miles out." Rusty looked up at him, his eyes cold. "In water more'n a mile deep."

Jesse looked back toward the trawler and saw Charlie Noble pulling the dinghy closer as the trawler slowly increased speed.

"We'll meet up with Deputy Clyde before he gets to where there might be anything left of that go-fast boat," Rusty explained. "Old Charlie's gonna make his way back through the sound and keep his mouth shut in exchange for the dinghy. Russ is explainin' all this to the women."

"You forgot about Suzanne," Jesse said. "How is it that we have her?" He pointed at the trawler, nearly a mile away. "And the main suspects in the kidnapping—no, no, the *only* other boat on radar out here, is heading east?"

Rusty grinned. "Charlie snuck her off in the dinghy when they weren't lookin'."

"You think they'll buy that?" Jesse asked, doubtfully. "What about the Coast Guard?"

"We're five miles from shore, bro," Rusty said. "Two miles outside his jurisdiction. When that deputy gets here, the primary thing will be to get Suzanne safely home. We'll tell him that's why we got her and not Charlie Noble. That trawler'll be long gone before the Coasties arrive."

"And if they chase it?" Jesse said. "They'll definitely have radar and a cutter's faster than that trawler."

Rusty looked out toward *Nauti Gull*, now nothing more than a dot on the horizon. "By the time they get that far out, they'll need a sub to catch her."

Chapter Thirty-Nine

———◆———◆———◆———◆———

Clyde *had* stopped to pick up Andy, leaving a neighbor to look after the boy, and by the time the two deputies reached *Dauntless*, they'd already learned what had happened from Russ over the radio, and Andy had agreed to escort *Dauntless* back to Russ's dock.

The nearest thing to medical care on the island was the school nurse and a midwife, who Andy had his dispatcher contact to come and have a look at Suzanne.

She'd been waiting at the dock, along with several other people, and Suzanne had been hurried across the yard and into the house. Russ had turned to Natalie and asked her to fetch Russel Junior from the neighbor's house and keep an eye on him until he could make sure his wife was okay.

He came out ten minutes later, headed straight toward the shop.

"What's goin' on?" Rusty asked as he and Jesse trotted to catch up.

Russ flung the door open. "Son of a bitch!"

They followed him inside to find all the cabinets opened and stuff lying all over the floor.

"They stole the silver?" Jesse asked, looking around at the tubs dumped on the floor.

"Every bit of it," Russ said. "Gone. Suzanne was right here, cleaning the gold chain when she saw the go-fast boat. That guy Tim caught her at the bottom of the steps up to the house and threatened to kill Russel, Junior. "

"How's Suzanne?" Pap asked him.

Russ turned to face them. "She'll be okay. The big guy roughed her up a little." He turned to Pap. "Thank you for stopping him."

Rusty had told Jesse what happened when they boarded. Russ and Rusty had gone straight into the main cabin through the glass doors, but Pap had gone up the starboard side deck, encountering Ringo Thomas as he was exiting the pilothouse with a pistol in his hand and the gold chain in the other.

Rusty had just entered the pilothouse from the rear as Russ went down to the lower deck, searching for Suzanne. Rusty told him how Pap had not only taken the gun and gold chain away from the guy, but when he'd tried to throw a punch, Pap had ducked under it, then thrown the guy overboard.

Russ had found Suzanne, along with Moose, in the master stateroom below the pilothouse. She'd been thrown onto the bed, bound, and the big man was standing over her, hunched over to avoid hitting his head on the ceiling. Russ had jumped on the bigger man, but had almost been knocked out when Moose thrust himself upward, jamming Russ's head into the ceiling.

That was when Pap and Rusty came in. Pap punched the bigger man in the heart with a powerful overhand right, and the giant had simply crumpled to the deck.

"They left us no choice," Pap told Russ. "Live by the sword...."

"What now?" Rusty asked.

"Andy's still talking to Suze," he replied. "She'll stick to the story. I don't know about Charlie Noble, though."

They'd been more than eight miles south of Ocracoke Inlet when the old man had set the trawler's autopilot and broke off one of the boat's through-hull fittings. The dinghy probably wasn't as fast as *Dauntless*, so Jesse figured Noble would be getting back to his boat soon.

"I'll go talk to him," he said, as Natalie and Russel Junior came in.

Russ scooped the boy up. "Let's go see your mommy, little man."

They followed Russ out, and Jesse continued around the house.

"Where are you going?" Natalie asked, trotting up beside him.

"I have to go see that old man, Charlie Noble."

She took his arm, stopping him, and turning him toward her. "You're not going to hurt him, are you?"

"I just want to talk to him," Jesse replied.

"I'm going with you."

"No, I think you should..."

She turned and went around to the passenger side of the Jeep, then climbed in.

Jesse sighed and rolled his eyes, but climbed in the driver's seat.

They rode out to the main highway in silence, and as they passed the entrance to the airport, she turned in her seat and looked at him. "You killed two men."

Jesse nodded somberly. "Those two men died the way they lived. I was just the instrument."

"Is that what you tell yourself?"

He glanced over and shook his head. "My conscience is clear. Both of them fired first."

"But you waited for them to fire," she said. "You're better trained."

He nodded. "And if Russ, Rusty, Pap, and I hadn't been trained, it's likely we'd be dead. You too." He paused and looked over at her again when he reached a stop sign. "Or worse."

She turned in her seat and looked forward again.

"Look," Jesse said, as he pulled into the parking lot, "those men were drug smugglers, and they were probably guilty of other crimes. That's a violent world. You don't see many criminals who are old, and most die a violent death. If it wasn't me, then it would've eventually been someone else. And between now and then, how many more innocent people would they have hurt?"

He parked the Jeep, and they climbed out, then started walking toward the docks.

"And you're okay knowing that?" she finally asked.

"Yes," Jesse replied, beginning to believe it himself. "When good and evil collide, only one can prevail. I'm not the kind of man who would stand aside and let someone be hurt."

They walked out onto the dock, and Natalie pointed out the old man's boat. Not that she needed to. It was the only boat in the marina with two dinghies; one of them brand-new.

"Charlie Noble?" Jesse called out, as they stopped beside the boat.

The old man's head appeared in the companionway. "I swear, I had no idea what they was doin'. Maybe I shoulda figured it out when that Cigarette boat met us outside the inlet. I thought the guy was just some rich businessman wantin' to buy Hal's boat."

"Permission to come aboard?" Jesse asked, but didn't wait for a response, and just stepped over the side and dropped down into the cockpit.

Natalie joined him.

"The woman they kidnapped is the wife of a very good friend of mine," Jesse said, his voice low and menacing. "She's a local."

"Yeah, I know," Noble said, tentatively coming up the ladder.

Jesse stepped back, keeping Natalie behind him just in case.

"I don't want no trouble with anyone," Noble said. "Especially the locals. I didn't know those guys were drug runners until I saw that blue boat."

Jesse looked back at the two dinghies tied to the stern. "What's that thing worth?"

Noble glanced back at the dinghy. "The engine alone's worth two hundred," he replied. "Another two for the boat. It's almost new."

Jesse studied the man's face for a moment. His skin was dark, with lines etched deeply in his face. His clothes were mostly rags, and his limbs were thin and sinewy. He'd lived a hard life, at least for the last several years.

Jesse pulled his wallet from his pocket and opened it. "Here," he said, extending a hundred-dollar-bill toward the man. This is for me pointing a rifle at you."

The man reached slowly for the bill, but when he took it, Jesse didn't let go.

"Keep in mind," he said softly, "that what I did to your friend out there, I can do from half a mile away. You talk, and you'll never even see me or know I was close."

He released the bill, then stepped back over to the dock, extending a hand to Natalie.

"And get rid of one of those dinghies," he told the old man. "Having two looks conspicuous."

He and Natalie walked back toward the parking lot and when they reached the Jeep, she climbed in and asked, "Do you think he'll keep quiet?"

"Yes," Jesse replied. "I believed him."

"So what now?" she asked, as Jesse backed out.

"I think Rusty and I are going to head back to the base," Jesse replied, as he drove away. "Or maybe I'll just fly home with Pap and do some fishing; the cobia run is just starting. And Henry invited Pap and I out to the Bahamas. I don't know. I just don't see this visit continuing the way we thought."

He shifted to third gear and left his hand resting on the shifter.

Natalie put her hand on top of his. "Do you have to go?" she asked him. "Maybe your friend can give your grandfather a ride back and you can stay for a few days."

Jesse shook his head. "After what she's been through, I don't want to put Suzanne out."

He looked over at her and she smiled. "The Silver Lake Inn always has rooms available for locals."

The End

Afterword

Whoa! I didn't see that ending coming.

I write linearly, completely freestyle, with no outline or even an idea of what the story will be about, how it ends, or what will happen. When I write, I don't even know what the next paragraph will be, much the same as one would read a story. It's called discovery writing or "pantsing" in some circles.

However, I do know a couple of things when I start a new story. I know when and where it will take place. I have to know those two things, so I'll be sure to get certain things like the sun and moon correct.

But what little I do plan doesn't always remain the same once the words start flowing. In *Fallen Hunter*, I never intended any part of the book to take place in Cuba, but a good bit of it did.

In this series, I can't deviate very much. These stories take place in the past and the past is written, quite literally. I have a document on my computer with Jesse's full biography from birth to retirement from the Marine Corps, including dates of significant life events, deployments, and promotions. It's been compiled over the years, as things came up in my books, so I can pretty much tell you where he was at any given time up to that point. All the details from his retirement to the present are in my book notes for each title.

When I decided to do this series, I went through Jesse's bio, knowing that he'd have four weeks of leave every year, and found places where Jesse would be or easily visit while on leave that I'd like to write about. Then I added breaks in the bio with book titles and ideas. I already have books A through G in his bio.

If you haven't caught on yet, the titles in this series will be in alphabetical order.

A Seller's Market

Bad Blood

Cocaine Cowboys

Done Deal and *Everglades Echo* will be coming in 2026.

The continued interest of my readers is the primary reason I keep making up these stories, and I hope you enjoy these glimpses back in time when Jesse, Rusty, and Billy were young.

Thank you, Greta, for the ideas and support, and for just being you, my one constant in life. We've had our lows and bad times but made it through to the other side every time. Thanks also to our kids and grandkids. It's for you that we work so hard.

Much appreciation to my technical advisors, Mike Ramsey, Katy McKnight, Alan Fader, Deg Priest, Jason Hebert, Drew Mutch, Ron Ramey, and Dana Vihlen, who provided valuable feedback on the manuscript's first draft.

Thanks also to my editor, Marsha Zinberg, my proofreader, Donna Rich, my narrator, Nick Sullivan, and my team at Down

Island Press and Aurora Publicity, who have all helped to transform the words of my story into what passes for a novel.

Now, I'm back to working on *Down Island*, the thirtieth novel in the Jesse McDermitt saga. I'm about ankle deep in it now.

Wayne

ALSO BY WAYNE STINNETT

The Jerry Snyder Caribbean Mystery Series

Wayward Sons   Vodou Child   Friends of the Devil

The Charity Styles Caribbean Thriller Series

Merciless Charity   Enduring Charity   Elusive Charity
Ruthless Charity   Vigilant Charity   Liable Charity
Reckless Charity   Lost Charity

The Jesse McDermitt Tropical Adventure Series16

A Seller's Market   Bad Blood   Cocaine Cowboys

The Jesse McDermitt Caribbean Adventure Series

Fallen Out   Rising Storm   Steady as She Goes
Fallen Palm   Rising Fury   All Ahead Full
Fallen Hunter   Rising Force   Man Overboard
Fallen Pride   Rising Charity   Cast Off
Fallen Mangrove   Rising Water   Fish On!
Fallen King   Rising Spirit   Weigh Anchor
Fallen Honor   Rising Thunder   Swift and Silent
Fallen Tide   Rising Warrior   Apalach Affair
Fallen Angel   Rising Moon   Dominica Blue
Fallen Hero   Rising Tide   Down Island

Rainbow of Collars Motivational Non-fiction Series

Blue Collar to No Collar   No Collar to Tank Top

The Gaspar's Revenge Ship's Store is open.

There, you can purchase all kinds of swag
related to my books.
You can find it at
WWW.GASPARS-REVENGE.COM